the city
of
the living

the city
of
the living

AND OTHER STORIES

by wallace stegner

Short Story Index Reprint Series

BOOKS FOR LIBRARIES PRESS
FREEPORT, NEW YORK

The following stories appeared originally in *Harper's Magazine*, "The Blue-Winged Teal," "The Traveler," "Pop Goes the Alley Cat," and "Maiden in a Tower"; "Field Guide to the Western Birds" first appeared in *New Short Novels*, 2, published by Ballantine Books, Inc.; "The City of the Living" and "The Volunteer" are reprinted by permission of *Mademoiselle*; "Impasse" is reprinted by permission of *Woman's Day*, the A & P Magazine.

STANDARD BOOK NUMBER:
8369-3028-2

LIBRARY OF CONGRESS CATALOG CARD NUMBER:
73-81276

MANUFACTURED BY
HALLMARK LITHOGRAPHERS, INC.
IN THE U.S.A.

contents

the city
of
the living

the
blue-winged
teal

STILL IN WADERS, with the string of ducks across his shoulder, he stood hesitating on the sidewalk in the cold November wind. His knees were stiff from being cramped up all day in the blind, and his feet were cold. Today, all day, he had been alive; now he was back ready to be dead again.

Lights were on all up and down the street, and there was a rush of traffic and a hurrying of people past and around him, yet the town was not his own, the people passing were strangers, the sounds of evening in this place were no sounds that carried warmth or familiarity. Though he had spent most of his twenty years in the town, knew hundreds of its people, could draw maps of its streets from memory, he wanted to admit familiarity with none of it. He had shut himself off.

Then what was he doing here, in front of this poolhall, loaded down with nine dead ducks? What had possessed him in the first place to borrow gun and waders and car from his father and go hunting? If he had wanted to breathe freely for a change, why hadn't he kept right on going? What was there in this place to draw him back? A hunter had to have a lodge to bring his meat to and people who would be glad of his skill. He had this poolhall and his father, John Lederer, Prop.

He stepped out of a woman's path and leaned against the door. Downstairs, in addition to his father, he would find old Max Schmeckebier, who ran a cheap blackjack game in the room under the sidewalk. He would find Giuseppe Sciutti, the Sicilian barber, closing his shop or tidying up the rack of *Artists and Models* and *The Nudist* with which he lured trade. He would probably find Billy Hammond, the night clerk from the Windsor Hotel, having his sandwich and beer and pie, or moving alone around a pool table, whistling abstractedly, practicing shots. If the afternoon blackjack game had broken up, there would be Navy Edwards, dealer and bouncer for Schmeckebier. At this time of evening there might be a few counter customers and a cop collecting his tribute of a beer or that other tribute that Schmeckebier paid to keep the cardroom open.

And he would find, sour contrast with the bright sky and the wind of the tule marshes, the cavelike room with its back corners in darkness, would smell that smell compounded of steam heat and cue-chalk dust, of sodden butts in cuspidors, of coffee and meat and beer smells from the counter, of cigarette smoke so unaired that it darkened the· walls. From anywhere back of the middle tables there would be the pervasive reek of toilet disinfectant. Back of the counter his father would be presiding, throwing the poolhall light switch to save a few cents when the place was empty, flipping it on to give an air of brilliant and successful use when feet came down the stairs past Sciutti's shop.

The hunter moved his shoulder under the weight of the

ducks, his mind full for a moment with the image of his father's face, darkly pale, fallen in on its bones, and the pouched, restless, suspicious eyes that seemed always looking for someone. Over the image came the face of his mother, dead now and six weeks buried. His teeth clicked at the thought of how she had held the old man up for thirty years, kept him at a respectable job, kept him from slipping back into the poolroom-Johnny he had been when she married him. Within ten days of her death he had hunted up this old failure of a poolhall.

In anger the hunter turned, thinking of the hotel room he shared with his father. But he had to eat. Broke as he was, a student yanked from his studies, he had no choice but to eat on the old man. Besides, there were the ducks. He felt somehow that the thing would be incomplete unless he brought his game back for his father to see.

His knees unwilling in the stiff waders, he went down the steps, descending into the light shining through Joe Sciutti's door, and into the momentary layer of clean bay rum smell, talcum smell, hair tonic smell, that rose past the still-revolving barber pole in the angle of the stairs.

Joe Sciutti was sweeping wads of hair from his tile floor, and hunched over the counter beyond, their backs to the door, were Schmeckebier, Navy Edwards, Billy Hammond, and an unknown customer. John Lederer was behind the counter, mopping alertly with a rag. The poolroom lights were up bright, but when Lederer saw who was coming he flipped the switch and dropped the big room back into dusk.

As the hunter came to the end of the counter their heads turned toward him. "Well I'm a son of a bee," Navy Edwards said, and scrambled off his stool. Next to him Billy Hammond half stood up so that his pale yellow hair took a halo from the backbar lights. "Say!" Max Schmeckebier said. "Say, dot's goot, dot's pooty goot, Henry!"

But Henry was watching his father so intently he did not turn to them. He slid the string of ducks off his shoulder and swung them up onto the wide walnut bar. They landed solidly — offering or tribute or ransom or whatever they were. For a moment it was as if this little act were private between the two of them. He felt queerly moved, his stomach tightened in suspense or triumph. Then the old man's pouchy eyes slipped from his and the old man came quickly forward along the counter and laid hands on the ducks.

He handled them as if he were petting kittens, his big white hands stringing the heads one by one from the wire.

"Two spoonbill," he said, more to himself than to others crowding around. "Shovelducks. Don't see many of those any more. And two, no three, hen mallards and one drake. Those make good eating."

Schmeckebier jutted his enormous lower lip. Knowing him for a stingy, crooked, suspicious little man, Henry almost laughed at the air he could put on, the air of a man of probity about to make an honest judgment in a dispute between neighbors. "I take a budderball," he said thickly. "A liddle budderball, dot is vot eats goot."

An arm fell across Henry's shoulders, and he turned his head to see the hand with red hairs rising from its pores, the wristband of a gray silk shirt with four pearl buttons. Navy Edwards' red face was close to his. "Come clean now," Navy said. "You shot 'em all sitting, didn't you, Henry?"

"I just waited till they stuck their heads out of their holes and let them have it," Henry said.

Navy walloped him on the back and convulsed himself laughing. Then his face got serious again, and he bore down on Henry's shoulder. "By God you could've fooled me," he said. "If I'd been makin' book on what you'd bring in I'd've lost my shirt."

"Such a pretty shirt, too," Billy Hammond said.

Across the counter John Lederer cradled a little drab duck in his hand. Its neck, stretched from the carrier, hung far down, but its body was neat and plump and its feet were waxy. Watching the sallow face of his father, Henry thought it looked oddly soft.

"Ain't that a beauty, though?" the old man said. "There ain't a prettier duck made than a blue-wing teal. You can have all your wood ducks and redheads, all the flashy ones." He spread a wing until the hidden band of bright blue showed. "Pretty?" he said, and shook his head and laughed suddenly, as if he had not expected to. When he laid the duck down beside the others his eyes were bright with sentimental moisture.

So now, Henry thought, you're right in your element. You always did want to be one of the boys from the poolroom pouring out to see the elk on somebody's running board, or leaning on a bar with a schooner of beer talking baseball or telling the boys about the big German Brown somebody brought in in a cake of ice. We haven't any elk or German Browns right now, but we've got some nice ducks, a fine display along five feet of counter. And who brought them in? The student, the alien son. It must gravel you.

He drew himself a beer. Several other men had come in, and he saw three more stooping to look in the door beyond Sciutti's. Then they too came in. Three tables were going; his father had started to hustle, filling orders. After a few minutes Schmeckebier and Navy went into the card room with four men. The poolroom lights were up bright again, there was an ivory click of balls, a rumble of talk. The smoke-filled air was full of movement.

Still more people dropped in, kids in high school athletic sweaters and bums from the fringes of skid road. They all stopped to look at the ducks, and Henry saw glances at his waders, heard questions and answers. John Lederer's boy. Some of them spoke to him, deriving importance from contact with him. A fellowship was promoted by the ducks strung out along the counter. Henry felt it himself. He was so mellowed by the way they spoke to him that when the players at the first table thumped with their cues, he got off his stool to rack them up and collect their nickels. It occurred to him that he ought to go to the room and get into a bath, but he didn't want to leave yet. Instead he came back to the counter and slid the nickels toward his father and drew himself another beer.

"Pretty good night tonight," he said. The old man nodded and slapped his rag on the counter, his eyes already past Henry and fixed on two youths coming in, his mouth fixing itself for the greeting and the "Well, boys, what'll it be?"

Billy Hammond wandered by, stopped beside Henry a moment. "Well, time for my nightly wrestle with temptation," he said.

"I was just going to challenge you to a game of call-shot."

"Maybe tomorrow," Billy said, and let himself out carefully as if afraid a noise would disturb someone — a mild, gentle, golden-haired boy who looked as if he ought to be in some prep school learning to say "Sir" to grownups instead of clerking in a girlie hotel. He was the only one of the poolroom crowd that Henry half liked. He thought he understood Billy Hammond a little.

He turned back to the counter to hear his father talking

with Max Schmeckebier. "I don't see how we could on this rig. That's the hell of it, we need a regular oven."

"In my room in back," Schmeckebier said. "Dot old electric range."

"Does it work?"

"Sure. Vy not? I t'ink so."

"By God," John Lederer said. "Nine ducks, that ought to give us a real old-fashioned feed." He mopped the counter, refilled a coffee cup, came back to the end and pinched the breast of a duck, pulled out a wing and looked at the band of blue hidden among the drab feathers. "Just like old times, for a change," he said, and his eyes touched Henry's in a look that might have meant anything from a challenge to an apology.

Henry had no desire to ease the strain that had been between them for months. He did not forgive his father the poolhall, or forget the way the old man had sprung back into the old pattern, as if his wife had been a jailer and he was now released. He neither forgot nor forgave the redhaired woman who sometimes came to the poolhall late at night and waited on a bar stool while the old man closed up. Yet now when his father remarked that the ducks ought to be drawn and plucked right away, Henry got to his feet.

"I could do ten while you were doing one," his father said.

The blood spread hotter in Henry's face, but he bit off what he might have said. "All right," he said. "You do them and I'll take over the counter for you."

So here he was, in the poolhall he had passionately sworn he would never do a lick of work in, dispensing Mrs. Morrison's meat pies and tamales smothered in chile, clumping behind the counter in the waders which had been the sign of his temporary freedom. Leaning back between orders, watching the Saturday night activity of the place, he half understood why he had gone hunting, and why it had seemed to him essential that he bring his trophies back here.

That somewhat disconcerted understanding was still troubling him when his father came back. The old man had put on a clean apron and brushed his hair. His pouched eyes, brighter and less houndlike than usual, darted along the bar, counting, and darted across the bright tables, counting again. His eyes met Henry's, and both smiled. Both of them, Henry thought, were a little astonished.

Later, propped in bed in the hotel room, he put down the magazine he had been reading and stared at the drawn blinds, the sleazy drapes, and asked himself why he was here. The story he had told others, and himself, that his mother's death had interrupted his school term and he was waiting for the new term before going back, he knew to be an evasion. He was staying because he couldn't get away, or wouldn't. He hated his father, hated the poolhall, hated the people he was thrown with. He made no move to hobnob with them, or hadn't until tonight, and yet he deliberately avoided seeing any of the people who had been his friends for years. Why?

He could force his mind to the barrier, but not across it. Within a half minute he found himself reading again, diving deep, and when he made himself look up from the page he stared for a long time at his father's bed, his father's shoes under the bed, his father's soiled shirts hanging in the open closet. All the home he had any more was this little room. He could not pretend that as long as he stayed here the fragments of his home and family were held together. He couldn't fool himself that he had any function in his father's life any more, or his father in his, unless his own hatred and his father's uneasy suspicion were functions. He ought to get out and get a job until he could go back to school. But he didn't.

Thinking made him sleepy, and he knew what that was, too. Sleep was another evasion, like the torpor and monotony of his life. But he let drowsiness drift over him, and drowsily he thought of his father behind the counter tonight, vigorous and jovial, Mine Host, and he saw that the usual fretful petulance had gone from his face.

He snapped off the bed light and dropped the magazine on the floor. Then he heard the rain, the swish and hiss of traffic in the wet street. He felt sad and alone, and he disliked the coldness of his own isolation. Again he thought of his father, of the failing body that had once been tireless and bull-strong, of the face before it had sagged and grown dewlaps of flesh on the square jaws. He thought of the many failures, the jobs that never quite worked out, the schemes that never quite paid off, and of the eyes that could not quite meet, not quite hold, the eyes of his cold son.

Thinking of this, and remembering when they had been a family and when his mother had been alive to hold them together, he felt pity, and he cried.

His father's entrance awakened him. He heard the fumbling at the door, the creak, the quiet click, the footsteps that groped in darkness, the body that bumped into something and halted, getting its bearings. He heard the sighing weight of his father's body on the bed, his father's sighing breath as he bent to untie his shoes. Feigning sleep, he lay unmoving, breathing deeply and steadily, but an anguish of fury had leaped in him as sharp and sudden as a sudden fear, for he smelled the smells his father brought with him: wet wool, stale tobacco, liquor; and above all, more penetrating than any, spreading through the room and polluting everything there, the echo of cheap musky perfume.

The control Henry imposed upon his body was like an ecstasy. He raged at himself for the weak sympathy that had troubled him all evening. One good night, he said to himself now, staring furiously upward. One lively Saturday night in the joint and he can't contain himself, he has to go top off the evening with his girl friend. And how? A drink in her room? A walk over to some illegal after-hours bar on Rum Alley? Maybe just a trip to bed, blunt and immediate?

His jaws ached from the tight clamping of his teeth, but his orderly breathing went in and out, in and out, while the old man sighed into bed and creaked a little, rolling over, and lay still. The taint of perfume seemed even stronger now. The sow must slop it on by the cupful. And so cuddly. Such a sugar baby. How's my old sweetie tonight? It's been too long since you came to see your baby. I should be real mad at you. The cheek against the lapel, the unreal hair against the collar, the perfume like some gaseous poison tainting the clothes it touched.

The picture of his mother's bureau drawers came to him, the careless simple collection of handkerchiefs and gloves and lace collars and cuffs, and he saw the dusty blue sachet packets and smelled the faint fragrance. That was all the scent she had ever used.

My God, he said, how can he stand himself?

After a time his father began to breathe heavily, then to snore. In the little prison of the room his breathing was obscene — loose and bubbling, undisciplined, animal. Henry with an effort relaxed his tense arms and legs, let himself sink. He tried to concentrate on his own breathing, but the other dominated him, burst out and died and whiffled and sighed again. By now he had a resolution in him like an iron bar. Tomorrow, for sure, for good, he would break out of his self-imposed isolation and see Frank, see Welby. They would lend him enough to get to the coast. Not another day in this hateful relationship. Not another night in this room.

He yawned. It must be late, two or three o'clock. He ought to get to sleep. But he lay uneasily, his mind tainted with hatred as the room was tainted with perfume. He tried cunningly to elude his mind, to get to sleep before it could notice, but no matter how he composed himself for blankness and shut his eyes and breathed deeply, his mind was out again in a half minute, bright-eyed, lively as a weasel, and he was helplessly hunted again from hiding place to hiding place.

Eventually he fell back upon his old device.

He went into a big dark room in his mind, a room shadowy with great half-seen tables. He groped and found a string above him and pulled, and light fell suddenly in a bright cone from the darker cone of the shade. Below the light lay an expanse of dark green cloth, and this was the only lighted thing in all that darkness. Carefully he gathered bright balls into a wooden triangle, pushing them forward until the apex lay over a round spot on the cloth. Quietly and thoroughly he chalked a cue: the inlaid handle and the smooth taper of the shaft were very real to his eyes and hands. He lined up the cue ball, aimed, drew the cue back and forth in smooth motions over the bridge of his left hand. He saw the balls run from the spinning shock of the break, and carom, and come to rest, and he hunted up·the yellow 1-ball and got a shot at it between two others. He had to cut it very fine, but he saw the shot go true, the 1 angle off cleanly into the side pocket. He saw the cue ball rebound and kiss and stop, and he shot the 2 in a straight shot for the left corner pocket, putting drawers on the cue ball to get shape for the 3.

Yellow and blue and red, spotted and striped, he shot pool balls into pockets as deep and black and silent as the cellars of his consciousness. He was not now quarry that his mind chased, but an actor, a willer, a doer, a man in command. By an act of will or of flight he focused his whole awareness on the game he played. His mind undertook it with intent concentration. He took pride in little two-cushion banks, little triumphs of accuracy, small successes of foresight. When he had finished one game and the green cloth was bare he dug the balls from the bin under the end of the table and racked them and began another.

Eventually, he knew, nothing would remain in his mind but the clean green cloth traced with running color and bounded by simple problems, and sometime in the middle of an intricately-planned combination shot he would pale off into sleep.

At noon, after the rain, the sun seemed very bright. It poured down from a clearing sky, glittered on wet roofs, gleamed in reflection from pavements and sidewalks. On the peaks beyond the city there was a purity of snow.

Coming down the hill Henry noticed the excessive brightness and could not tell whether it was really as it seemed, or whether his plunge out of the dark and isolated hole of his life had restored a lost capacity to see. A slavery, or a paralysis, was ended; he had been for three hours in the company of a friend; he had been eyed with concern; he had been warmed by solicitude and generosity. In his pocket he had fifty dollars, enough to get him to the coast and let him renew his life. It seemed to him incredible that he had alternated between dismal hotel and dismal poolroom so long. He could not understand why he had not before this moved his legs in the direction of the hill. He perceived that he had been sullen and morbid, and he concluded with some surprise that even Schmeckebier and Edwards and the rest might have found him a difficult companion.

His father too. The fury of the night before had passed, but he knew he would not bend again toward companionship. That antipathy was too deep. He would never think of his father again without getting the whiff of that perfume. Let him have it; it was what he wanted, let him have it. They could part without an open quarrel, maybe, but they would part without love. They could part right now, within an hour.

Two grimy stairways led down into the cellar from the alley he turned into. One went to the furnace room, the other to the poolhall. The iron rail was blockaded with filled ash cans. Descent into Avernus, he said to himself, and went down the left-hand stair.

The door was locked. He knocked, and after some time knocked again. Finally someone pulled on the door from inside. It stuck, and was yanked irritably inward. His father stood there in his shirt sleeves, a cigar in his mouth.

"Oh," he said. "I was wondering what had become of you."

The basement air was foul and heavy, dense with the reek from the toilets. Henry saw as he stepped inside that at the far end only the night light behind the bar was on, but that light was coming from Schmeckebier's door at this end too, the two weak illuminations diffusing in the shadowy poolroom, leaving the middle in almost absolute dark. It was the appropriate time, the appropriate place, the stink of his prison appropriately concentrated. He drew his lungs full of it with a kind of passion, and he said, "I just came down to — "

"Who is dot?" Schmeckebier called out. He came to his door, wrapped to the armpits in a bar apron, with a spoon in his hand, and he bent, peering out into the dusk like a disturbed dwarf in an underhill cave. "John? Who? Oh, Henry. Shust in time, shust in time. It is not long now." His lower lip waggled, and he pulled it up, apparently with an effort.

Henry said, "What's not long?"

"Vot?" Schmeckebier said, and thrust his big head far out. "You forgot about it?"

"I must have," Henry said.

"The duck feed," his father said impatiently.

They stood staring at one another in the dusk. The right moment was gone. With a little twitch of the shoulder Henry let it go. He would wait a while, pick his time. When Schmeckebier went back to his cooking, Henry saw through the doorway the lumpy bed, the big chair with a blanket folded over it, the roll-top desk littered with pots and pans, the green and white enamel of the range. A rich smell of roasting came out and mingled oddly with the chemical stink of toilet disinfectant.

"Are we going to eat in here" he asked.

His father snorted. "How could we eat in there? Old Maxie lived in the ghetto too damn long. By God I never saw such a boar's nest."

"Vot's duh matter? Vot's duh matter?" Schmeckebier said. His big lip thrust out, he stooped to look into the oven, and John Lederer went shaking his head up between the tables to the counter. Henry followed him, intending to make the break when he got the old man alone. But he saw the three plates set up on the bar, the three glasses of tomato juice, the platter of olives and celery, and he hesitated. His father reached with a salt shaker and shook a little salt into each glass of tomato juice.

"All the fixings," he said. "Soon as Max gets those birds out of the oven we can take her on."

Now it was easy to say, "As soon as the feed's over I'll be shoving off." Henry opened his mouth to say it, but was interrupted this time by a light tapping at the glass door beyond Sciutti's shop. He swung around angrily and saw duskily beyond the glass the smooth blond hair, the even smile.

"It's Billy," he said. "Shall I let him in?"

"Sure," the old man said. "Tell him to come in and have a duck with us."

But Billy Hammond shook his head when Henry asked him. He was shaking his head almost as he came through the door. "No thanks, I just ate. I'm full of chow mein. This is a family dinner anyway. You go on ahead."

"Got plenty," John Lederer said, and made a motion as if to set a fourth place at the counter.

"Who is dot?" Schmeckebier bawled from the back. "Who come in? Is dot Billy Hammond? Set him up a blate."

"By God his nose sticks as far into things as his lip," Lederer said. Still holding the plate, he roared back, "Catch up with the parade, for Christ sake, or else tend to your cooking." He looked at Henry and Billy and chuckled.

Schmeckebier had disappeared, but now his squat figure blotted the lighted doorway again. "Vot? Vot you say?"

"Vot?" John Lederer said. "Vot, vot, vot? Vot does it matter vot I said? Get the hell back to your kitchen."

He was, Henry saw, in a high humor. The effect of last

night was still with him. He was still playing Mine Host. He looked at the two of them and laughed so naturally that Henry almost joined him. "I think old Maxie's head is full of duck dressing," he said, and leaned on the counter. "I ever tell you about the time we came back from Reno together? We stopped off in the desert to look at a mine, and got lost on a little dirt road so we had to camp. I was trying to figure out where we were, and started looking for stars, but it was clouded over, hard to locate anything. So I ask old Maxie if he can see the Big Dipper anywhere. He thinks about that maybe ten minutes with his lip stuck out and then he says, 'I t'ink it's in duh water bucket.' "

He did the grating gutturals of Schmeckebier's speech so accurately that Henry smiled in spite of himself. His old man made another motion with the plate at Billy Hammond. "Better let me set you up a place."

"Thanks," Billy said. His voice was as polite and soft as his face, and his eyes had the ingenuous liquid softness of a girl's. "Thanks, I really just ate. You go on, I'll shoot a little pool if it's all right."

Now came Schmeckebier with a big platter held in both hands. He bore it smoking through the gloom of the pool-hall and up the steps to the counter, and John Lederer took it from him there and with a flourish speared one after another three tight-skinned brown ducks and slid them onto the plates set side by side for the feast. The one frugal light from the backbar shone on them as they sat down. Henry looked over his shoulder to see Billy Hammond pull the cord and flood a table with a sharp-edged cone of brilliance. Deliberately, already absorbed, he chalked a cue. His lips pursed, and he whistled, and whistling, bent to take aim.

Lined up in a row, they were not placed for conversation, but John Lederer kept attempting it, leaning forward over his plate to see Schmeckebier or Henry. He filled his mouth with duck and dressing and chewed, shaking his head with pleasure, and snapped off a bite of celery with a crack like a breaking stick. When his mouth was clear he leaned and said to Schmeckebier, "Ah, das schmeckt gut, hey Maxie?"

"Ja," Schmeckebier said, and sucked grease off his lip and only then turned in surprise. "Say, you speak German?"

"Sure, I speak German," Lederer said. "I worked three weeks once with an old squarehead brickmason that taught me the whole language. He taught me about sehr gut and nicht wahr and besser I bleiben right hier, and he always had his frau make me up a lunch full of kalter aufschnitt and gemixte pickeln. I know all about German."

Schmeckebier stared a moment, grunted, and went back to his eating. He had already stripped the meat from the bones and was gnawing the carcass.

"Anyway," John Lederer said, "es schmeckt God damn good." He got up and went around the counter and drew a mug of coffee from the urn. "Coffee?" he said to Henry.

"Please."

His father drew another mug and set it before him. "Maxie?"

Schmeckebier shook his head, his mouth too full for talk. For a minute, after he had set out two little jugs of cream, Lederer stood as if thinking. He was watching Billy Hammond move quietly around the one lighted table, whistling. "Look at that sucker," Lederer said. "I bet he doesn't even know where he is."

By the time he got around to his stool he was back at the German. "Schmeckebier," he said. "What's that mean?"

"Uh?"

"What's your name mean? Tastes beer? Likes beer?"

Schmeckebier rolled his shoulders. The sounds he made

eating were like sounds from a sty. Henry was half sickened, sitting next to him, and he wished the old man would let the conversation drop. But apparently it had to be a feast, and a feast called for chatter.

"That's a hell of a name, you know it?" Lederer said, and already he was up again and around the end of the counter. "You couldn't get into any church with a name like that." His eyes fastened on the big drooping greasy lip, and he grinned.

"Schmeckeduck, that ought to be your name," he said. "What's German for duck? Vogel? Old Man Schmecke-vogel. How about number two?"

Schmeckebier pushed his plate forward and Lederer forked a duck out of the steam table. Henry did not take a second.

"You ought to have one," his father told him. "You don't get grub like this every day."

"One's my limit," Henry said.

For a while they worked at their plates. Back of him Henry heard the clack of balls hitting, and a moment later the rumble as a ball rolled down the chute from a pocket. The thin, abstracted whistling of Billy Hammond broke off, became words:

> Annie doesn't live here any more.
> You must be the one she waited for.
> She said I would know you by the blue in your eye —

"Talk about one being your limit," his father said. "When we lived in Nebraska we used to put on some feeds. You remember anything about Nebraska at all?"

"A little," Henry said. He was irritated at being dragged into reminiscences, and he did not want to hear how many ducks the town hog could eat at a sitting.

"We'd go out, a whole bunch of us," John Lederer said. "The sloughs were black with ducks in those days. We'd come back with a buggyful, and the womenfolks'd really put us on a feed. Fifteen, twenty, thirty people. Take a hundred ducks to fill 'em up." He was silent a moment, staring across the counter, chewing. Henry noticed that he had tacked two wings of a teal up on the frame of the backbar mirror, small, strong bows with a band of bright blue half hidden in them. The old man's eyes slanted over, caught Henry's looking at the wings.

"Doesn't seem as if we'd had a duck feed since we left there," he said. His forehead wrinkled; he rubbed his neck, leaning forward over his plate, and his eyes met Henry's in the backbar mirror. He spoke to the mirror, ignoring the gobbling image of Schmeckebier between his own reflection and Henry's.

"You remember that set of china your mother used to have? The one she painted herself? Just the plain white china with the one design on each plate?"

Henry sat stiffly, angry that his mother's name should even be mentioned between them in this murky hole, and after what had passed. Gabble, gabble, gabble, he said to himself. If you can't think of anything else to gabble about, gabble about your dead wife. Drag her through the poolroom too. Aloud he said, "No, I guess I don't."

"Blue-wing teal," his father said, and nodded at the wings tacked to the mirror frame. "Just the wings, like that. Awful pretty. She thought a teal was about the prettiest little duck there was."

His vaguely rubbing hand came around from the back of his neck and rubbed along the cheek, pulling the slack flesh and distorting the mouth. Henry said nothing, watching the pouched hound eyes in the mirror.

It was a cold, skin-tightening shock to realize that the hound eyes were cloudy with tears. The rubbing hand went over them, shaded them like a hatbrim, but the mouth below remained distorted. With a plunging movement his father was off the stool.

"Oh, God damn!" he said in a strangling voice, and went past Henry on hard, heavy feet, down the steps and pɛ t Billy Hammond, who neither looked up nor broke the sad thin whistling.

Schmeckebier had swung around. "Vot's duh matter? Now vot's duh matter?"

With a short shake of the head, Henry turned away from him, staring after his father down the dark poolhall. He felt as if orderly things were breaking and flying apart in his mind; he had a moment of white blind terror that this whole scene upon whose reality he counted was really only a dream, something conjured up out of the bottom of his consciousness where he was accustomed to comfort himself into total sleep. His mind was still full of the anguished look his father had hurled at the mirror before he ran.

The hell with you, the look had said. The hell with you, Schmeckebier, and you, my son Henry. The hell with your ignorance, whether you're stupid or whether you just don't know all you think you know. You don't know enough to kick dirt down a hole. You know nothing at all, you know less than nothing because you know things wrong.

He heard Billy's soft whistling, saw him move around his one lighted table — a well-brought-up boy from some suburban town, a polite soft gentle boy lost and wandering among pimps and prostitutes, burying himself for some reason among people who never even touched his surface. Did he shoot pool in his bed at night, tempting sleep, as

Henry did? Did his mind run carefully to angles and banks and englishes, making a reflecting mirror of them to keep from looking through them at other things?

Almost in terror he looked out across the sullen cave, past where the light came down in an intense isolated cone above Billy's table, and heard the lugubrious whistling that went on without intention of audience, a recurrent and deadening and only half-conscious sound. He looked toward the back, where his father had disappeared in the gloom, and wondered if in his bed before sleeping the old man worked through a routine of little jobs: cleaning the steam table, ordering a hundred pounds of coffee, jacking up the janitor about the mess in the hall. He wondered if it was possible to wash yourself to sleep with restaurant crockery, work yourself to sleep with chores, add yourself to sleep with columns of figures, as you could play yourself to sleep with a pool cue and a green table and fifteen colored balls. For a moment, in the sad old light with the wreckage of the duck feast at his elbow, he wondered if there was anything more to his life, or his father's life, or Billy Hammond's life, or anyone's life, than playing the careful games that deadened you into sleep.

Schmeckebier, beside him, was still groping in the fog of his mind for an explanation of what had happened. "Vere'd he go?" he said, and nudged Henry fiercely. "Vot's duh matter?"

Henry shook him off irritably, watching Billy Hammond's oblivious bent head under the light. He heard Schmeckebier's big lip flop and heard him sucking his teeth.

"I tell you," the guttural voice said. "I got somet'ing dot fixes him if he feels bum."

He too went down the stairs past the lighted table and

into the gloom at the back. The light went on in his room, and after a minute or two his voice was shouting, "John! Say, come here, uh? Say, John!"

Eventually John Lederer came out of the toilet and they walked together between the tables. In his fist Schmecke-bier was clutching a square bottle. He waved it in front of Henry's face as they passed, but Henry was watching his father. He saw the crumpled face, oddly rigid, like the face of a man in the grip of a barely controlled rage, but his father avoided his eyes.

"Kümmel," Schmeckebier said. He set four ice cream dishes on the counter and poured three about a third full of clear liquor. His squinted eyes lifted and peered toward Billy Hammond, but Henry said, on an impulse, "Let him alone. He's walking in his sleep."

So there were only the three. They stood together a moment and raised their glasses. "Happy days," John Lederer said automatically. They drank.

Schmeckebier smacked his lips, looked at them one after another, shook his head in admiration of the quality of his kümmel, and waddled back toward his room with the bottle. John Lederer was already drawing hot water to wash the dishes.

In the core of quiet which was not broken even by the clatter of crockery and the whistling of Billy Hammond, Henry said what he had to say. "I'll be leaving," he said. "Probably tonight."

But he did not say it in anger, or with the cold command of himself that he had imagined in advance. He said it like a cry, and with the feeling he might have had on letting go the hand of a friend too weak and too exhausted to cling any longer to their inadequate shared driftwood in a wide cold sea.

anything that might demand his son's strength for a
er. Sitting on the tub's edge, he removed the ther
eter and read it. A hundred two and a half, exactl
t it had been since the night before.

e saw the boy's foot and skinny leg, the Achilles
on standing out from the heel, the long body jack
ed in an agony of cramps, and the feeling that came
r him was like the slipping of a knot or the fraying of a
e that had held something secure until then. He looked
horror at the way the disease had wasted his son in
ely more than a day, and he drew into his lungs the in-
man, poisonous stench of the sickness. That was the
ment when it first occurred to him that the boy could

The thermometer rattled in the glass of germicide as he
t it back. With an arm around the skinny shoulders he
lped the boy back to bed, where he fed chloromycetin
psules one by one into the obedient mouth and after each
e offered the water glass to the enameled lips. He
oothed the sheet and turned the pillow. "Now back to
eep," he said.

For a moment he continued to stare fascinated at the
asted face, the closed eyes. He was talking to a nothing,
a silence. The boy had folded back into the bed with a
ttle groan and had moved nothing but his lips since. The
ct of drawing the sheet up to his chin was so intimately
ssociated in the father's mind with the last act of a death-
ed that he ground his teeth. In one fierce grab he caught
mosquito that had got in under the net. Then he tucked in
he edges and tiptoed out. Looking back from the door
e felt guilt in him like a knife for all the things he might
have done and had failed to do. There was a darkness in

the city
of
the living

AT A CERTAIN moment he looked around him and was over-
come by a feeling almost like terror at how strange this
all was.

Not even the international familiarity of washbowl and
water closet, not even the familiar labels of pill bottles on
his table or the familiar carbolic reek of disinfectant, could
make him quite accept the fact that this was happening to
him and his son, and in this place. The darkened room
next door was real to him, and this bathroom with its iron
shutters open to night and the mosquitoes, but their reality
was an imprecise reality of nightmare. It was hard to keep
from believing that under the ghostly mosquito net in the
next room lay not his son but someone with a strange face,
or no face at all; and that in this tiled cell sat not himself but
some alien enduring an ordeal by light and silence.

Outside the window, across the tops of the palms whose
occasional dry clashing was the only sound he heard, were
the unseen minaret from which the muezzin had cried the
hour of prayer at the oncoming of dark, the unseen mud

houses of Moslems and Copts, the fluted lotus columns, the secret shine of the Nile, the mud flats spreading toward the rims that guarded the Valley of the Kings. Against his windows the ancient dark of Egypt sucked like the vacuum created by wind under a lee wall. It made him conscious of the beating of his heart.

Turning from the outside dark and the soft clash of palms, he listened at the bedroom door, opened it and slipped in. He could not see the face but only the vague shape under the net. Yet he thought he felt the fever through sheet and net and three feet of air, and when he slipped his hand under to touch the boy's forehead he felt how tentative and fearful a gesture that was.

The luminous hands of his watch showed only one thirty-five. More chloromycetin at two. He was tempted to get the thermometer and see if the heavy dosages since noon had brought the fever down at all. But it wouldn't be fair to wake the boy. He needed the sleep — if it *was* sleep.

Back in the bathroom with his eye to the narrowing crack of the door he watched the sickroom gather its darkness. The netted bed retreated, the shiny bathroom was restored to him, with the vacuum of night at its windows. He stepped out onto the narrow iron balcony, and as he did so something crashed and scrambled in the top of a palm on a level with the rail, almost in his face. Fright, and the thought that whatever it was had been crouched there looking in at him, froze him rigid; and he heard first the pound of his heart, then a small rustling, then silence, then the mosquitoes gathering with a thin whine around his head. Whatever had been among the palm fronds, rat or monkey or bird, was quiet. And there was no sound from the town either, not even the bark of a dog.

Above him the sky was the rich blue-black he had seen

in fine Persian rugs, with the Milky W
it and many brilliant dry stars. He t
watching their flocks by night and Aral
the cumbersome stone instruments of
and he looked for lights but saw only a
like a cigar end in the blackness beyond
City of the Dead had extended in tl
Thebes. He had no idea what it might
as enigmatic and watchful as himself on
stealthy neighbor in the palm top. Aft
Though he looked hard he saw not a gl
glimmer of a star, from the river sweepin

A fumbling from behind him sent his
the light chain above the washbowl, and
boy came in, blinking and stumbling, h
jamas with one hand, and groped numbly
on the toilet and was wracked with ex
With a groan he put his elbows on his kn
head in his hands; to his father's scared ey
tally skinny, his arms pipestems too weak f
hands. His face when he lifted it was pu
with fever and sleep but wasted to skeletor
the jaws.

The father held his hand against the bo
help the weak neck. The forehead was ver
glazed like agate. "Better now?"

The boy bent his head but sat still. In a n
wracked again. His stench was almost unbe
ing his breath against the smell, the father sh
thermometer and put it to the agate lips.
obediently, even in the midst of a spasm — h
obedient he was in his sickness — and the tw
boy absorbed with his inward war, the father

say a
answ
mon
wha
H
ten
kni
ove
rop
wit
bar
hu
mo
die

pu
he
ca
or
sr
sl

w
t
li
a
a
l

his mind where this only child had been. Already the memory of him was all but unbearable.

In the harsh light of the bathroom he felt trapped like an animal in a flashlight beam. The sight of his own trapped eyes glittering was an intense, dreamlike plausibility until he realized that he was looking into a mirror. Darkness would have been a relief, but not the darkness outside. He had a fantasy that the light and the unreal solidity of brass and porcelain, himself and the stench of his son's sickness, might all be sucked out into the night and lost. It was better to cling to this, to his separateness and identity, for somehow, at some totally unbearable crisis in his dream of personal pain and loss, he had a faith that he might waken and be saved.

In the end he found occupation in the routines of a sick-bed vigil. He scrubbed the toilet and dumped disinfectant in it, washed his hands a long time in germicidal water, drove the mosquitoes out of the room with the DDT bomb. But those jobs, treat them as carefully as he might, lasted him no more than twenty minutes. Then he was back again, caught between the light and the darkness, the only wakeful thing in all the dark city of Thebes except for the animal in the palm top and whoever was responsible for the red glow across the river. The thought of the light raised sudden goose flesh on him, as if grave robbers or vampires prowled there.

After a while he got out his briefcase and set about bringing his correspondence up to date. That morning he had filled his pen at the hotel desk. At the same time, as if with foresight, he had picked up a new supply of hotel stationery. He had Egyptian stamps folded into a slip of waxed paper in the briefcase. He comforted himself with his own efficient work habits, and he cleaned up several things:

A note to the American Express in Rome returning some unused railroad tickets for refund. A letter of recommendation for a junior colleague trying for a Government job. A word to his secretary saying briefly that illness had changed their plans so that it didn't look as if any mail should be sent to Athens at all. Send anything up to December first to Rome.

The three stamped and addressed envelopes gave him such satisfaction that he wished he had fifty to do. He addressed the two picture postcards he found and wished there were more. But if no more cards and no more details to clear up, then a personal letter or two. With a sheet of stationery before him and his full pen in his hand, his eyes a little scratchy from sleeplessness, he considered whom he should write to. Not instantly, but over a period of seconds or minutes, it occurred to him that there was no one.

Not for the kind of letter he wanted and feared to write. He had no family closer than cousins, strangers he had not seen for years. His wife was worse than a stranger — an enemy — and though he owed her reports on their son's health and a monthly alimony check he owed her no more than that, and from her he could expect nothing at all. Friends? To what golf companion or bridge companion or house-party acquaintance or business associate could he write a letter beginning, as it must, "My son is in the next room very sick, perhaps dying, with typhoid . . ." ?

He put his hands palms down on the desk and held them there a moment before he crumpled the sheet on which he had written the date and a confident "Dear . . ." *Dear who?*

I am sitting in the bathroom of a hotel in Luxor, Egypt, at nearly three in the morning, and I am just beginning to realize that here or anywhere else I am almost completely alone. I have spent my life avoiding entanglements. I breathed a sigh of relief when Ruth left. The only person I have cared about is this boy in the next room, and he is half a stranger. You should hear the machinery creak when we try to talk to each other. And I have to go and bring him into this rotten country where everybody is stuffed to the eyes with germs . . .

On a new sheet of paper he wrote, lifting his face while he tried to remember the figures, certain statistics on Egyptian public health he had read somewhere.

Trachoma	97 per cent
Bilharziasis	96 per cent
Syphilis	26 per cent
Tuberculosis	? per cent
Cholera?	
Typhoid?	

It seemed important to have them down. He wished he had clipped the newspaper or World Health report or whatever he had seen them in. For a moment's flash of memory he remembered Giles at the Mahdi Club in Cairo saying to him quietly as they waited for the boy to wipe off their bowls and hand them back, "Wash your hands in carbolic water after we go in. This kid's got a beautiful case of pinkeye." He saw himself quoting Egyptian health statistics to head-wagging men who dropped in to the office or to people who listened to him around grate fires. It's no joke, he heard himself say. Practically every Egyptian you see is one-eyed, and they've all got bilharzia worms. All the filth diseases, of course — cholera and typhoid are endemic. It was typhoid that nearly got Dan, you know, in Luxor.

He listened, hypnotized by the even, world-traveled voice, and raised a hand to brush away a mosquito and smelled the germicide, and said to himself that if the hotel doctor and the manager hadn't been decent Dan might be in a fever hospital right now instead of quarantined in this wing. He went back over his remarks, polishing them, and came to the word "nearly" and stopped.

The thing that he wanted to think about or write about as an adventure of the trip, successfully passed, rose up before him suddenly and blanked his whole mind with fear. Controlling himself, forcing the discipline, he picked up papers and one by one put them away in the briefcase, refolding the stamps into their waxed paper. Under some odds and ends of folders he found the return envelope of an insurance company. A premium due. With relief, escaping, he opened the checkbook and unscrewed the pen and wrote the check neatly and tore it out. It lay in his hand, a yellow slip like thousands he had written, a bond with the order and security of home. A checkbook wasn't any good here, of course, but in any good international bank on proper identification and after a reasonable delay, it would . . . they had to know who you were, that was all. Just a little of the machinery of security, a passport, letter of credit, the usual identifications, maybe filling out a form or two . . .

Robert Chapman, age forty-two; nationality, American; place of birth, Sacramento, California; residence, San Francisco; education, B.A. University of California, 1931. Married? Divorced. Children? One son, Daniel. Member Bohemian Club of San Francisco, Mill Valley Club, Kiwanis. Property: one-twelfth of a cooperative apartment house on Green Street, weekend cottage Carmel, certain bonds, Oldsmobile hard-top convertible. Income around eighteen thousand annually. Contributions: the usual good causes, Community Fund, Red Cross, Civil Liberties Union, the Sierra Club's conservation program. Insurance program the usual — forty thousand straight life plus annuity plan.

I believe in insurance, he told the smooth-faced, gray-haired man across the desk. Always have. My parents bought my first policy for me when I was ten, and I've added to it according to a careful plan from time to time. I've known too many people who were wiped out for lack of it. I carry a hundred thousand — fifty thousand on my car, plus all the rest except the freak stuff. Personal injury, property damage, collision, fire, theft — they all pay, even if you never have to collect on them. Real property too. My place at Carmel has comprehensive coverage, practically every sort of damage or accident — window breakage, hail, wind, fire, earthquake, falling airplanes. I carry a twenty-five-dollar deductible personal-property floater. It's indispensable, when you're traveling especially. Protects you wherever you are. Same with my health-plan membership. Anywhere in the world I'm protected on my medical and hospital bills.

For that matter, he said, smiling, my physician gave me some good advice before this last trip. He prescribed me a little kit of pills — penicillin tablets, empirin, sulfaguanidine, dramamine against travel sickness, chloromycetin and aureomycin in case we got sick anywhere out of reach of medical care and had a real emergency. I can tell you we were glad of that doctor's advice when we got way up the Nile, in Luxor, and my son Dan, in spite of inoculations and everything, came down with typhoid . . .

Neatly he folded the check and folded a sheet of stationery around it and the premium notice and put them in the return envelope, half irritated that they made it so easy. A man didn't mind addressing an envelope.

His face was greasy with sweat. Restlessly he rose and washed in cool water, looked at his shadowed eyes in the mirror, turned away, slipped into the bedroom and eased into the chair by the bedside. The breathings and the spasmodic small twitchings made the boy under the net seem utterly vulnerable somehow. In the dark, his eyes tiredly closed, he sat for an indefinite time seeing red shapes flow and change in the pocket of his lids. Among them, abruptly, coned with light like an operating table, appeared his son, dead, openmouthed, horribly wasted, and he awoke with a shudder and found his shirt clammy and his lungs laboring at the close air. His watch read twenty minutes to four.

To wait until four was impossible. He opened the bathroom door wide to let in light, and brought the capsules and a glass of water. The boy awoke at a touch, his dry lips working, his eyelids struggling open, and lifted his head weakly to swallow the medicine.

"How do you feel now? Better?"

"Hot," the stiff lips said.

"Would you like a damp towel on your eyes?"

"Yes."

The father slipped the thermometer into the boy's mouth and went into the bathroom. The disease-and-disinfectant smell was newly obnoxious to him as he wrung out the towel. When he returned, the boy had turned his head and the thermometer had slipped half out of his parted lips. With a swift searching of the emaciated face the father took it and held it to the light. At first the hairline of mercury would not reveal itself, and helpless anger shook him at people who would make an instrument no-body could read. Then he caught the glittering line, twisted carefully. Its end lay at 102°.

Down half a degree? Suspiciously he felt the forehead, but it was wet from the towel. The dry, slippery hands were still hot. But less hot than they had been? Or had the thermometer slipped out long enough to make the reading inaccurate?

Starting to take the temperature again, he stopped, and then he deliberately pulled down and tucked in the net. He did this, he knew, not out of reassured hope but out of cowardice. His heart had leaped so at that half degree of hope that he did not want to find he had been wrong. In a minute or two he was back in the bathroom, sitting at the table before his worthless and undemanding brief-case and the little pile of cards and envelopes. He felt ex-posed to all the eyes of Luxor; once, after the Long Beach earthquake in 1933, he had seen a man shaving in such a bathroom as this, with the whole outside wall peeled away, and he stood there before the mirror at ten o'clock on a Sunday morning, with his suspenders down and the world looking in. It was a ridiculous image. But he did not get up and pull down the shutters and close himself in.

His eyes were full of the pattern of square tile three feet before his eyes. He found that by squinting or widening his eyes he could make the squares begin to dissolve and spin in a vortex of glittering planes and reflections. When he wanted to he took hold again and forced the spinning to stop and the tiles to settle back to order. Then he nar-rowed his eyes again and watched the spinning recom-mence.

Some level of mind apart from his intense concentration told him, without heat, that he could hypnotize himself that way, and some other layer still deeper and more cunning smiled at that warning. He held the squares firmly in focus for a minute, stretched them, let them spin, brought them back under the discipline of will and eye, relaxed again and let them spin, enjoying the control he had of them and of himself. It was as if the whole back of his head was a hollow full of bees.

He was facing the blank wall and his neck was stiff. His head ached dully and his eyes were scratchy in the tired light of the bathroom. The muezzin was crying prayer again across the housetops of Thebes, the open shutters gave not on darkness but on gray twilight, and at the end of his reach of vision, against a sky palely lavender, he saw the minaret and the jutting balcony high up, and on the balcony the small black movement. He could distinguish no words in the rise and fall of the muezzin's cry; it was as empty of meaning as a yodel.

Stiffly he stretched and rolled his stiff neck. His left arm was sore from yesterday's reinoculation; the memory of his night's watch was like a memory of delirium. He felt pleased that it had passed, and looked at his watch. Five-thirty. His mind groped. And then the pretense of awakening to sane reality fell away, and he stood in the pale, overtaken electric light sick with shame at the trick he had played upon his own anxiety and responsibility. What if he had missed a time for the pills?

His flesh lay like putty on his bones. In the membranes of his mouth he tasted all the night's odors — the smell of sickness that was like no human or animal odor but virulent, deadly, and obscene; the smells of the things one relied on to stay alive, the disinfectant smell and the DDT spray. His arm was a swollen, throbbing ache. He belched and tasted bile, and bent to hold cool water in cupped handfuls against his eyes. When he took a drink from the carafe the chlorine bite of the halazone tablets gagged him. The effort, the steady, unrelieved, incessant effort that it took in this place to stay alive! He looked at his haggard, smudged face in the mirror and he hated Egypt with a kind of ecstasy. Finally, unwillingly, he went through the bedroom door.

Daybreak had not come here. The room was the vaguest gloom, yet when he turned on the light it had somehow the look that closed rooms have in daylight, a dissipated air like that of a room where a drunkard sleeps through the day. Shaking down the thermometer as he stepped across the rug, holding his breath to hear anything from the bed, the father approached and bent across the net. He bent his head lower, listening. "Dan?" he said. Then in a convulsive panic he tore away the net, knowing his son was dead.

The boy slept peacefully, lightly, his breathing even and soft. His forehead was cool to his father's shaking hand. There was no need for the thermometer: the fever was not merely down but gone. In his jubilation the father picked up the little vulture-headed image he had bought for the boy the first day and tossed it to the ceiling and caught it. He moved around the room, retrieved a horsehair fly whisk from the floor and hung it on the dresser post, eased the shutter up a little way for air. The boy slept on.

Outside in the hall he heard soft sounds, and going quickly to the door he surprised the hall boy depositing his shined shoes. The white eyes flashed upward in the face of the crouching figure, the bare feet moved respectfully backward a step, the long, belted robe swung like a dancer's.

"Saeeda," the soft voice whispered.

"Saeeda. Can I have tea?"

"Only tea?"

"Fruit, maybe. Oranges or plantains."

"Yes. How is your son?"

"Better," the father said, and knew that this was why he had opened the door, just for the chance of telling some-one. "Much better. The fever is gone."

The floor boy seemed genuinely pleased. After all, Chapman thought, he probably hadn't liked the business of be-ing quarantined and inoculated any better than anybody else. To an Egyptian typhoid normally meant, if not death, several weeks in a fever hospital and a long, feeble con-valescence. This one now was smiling and delighted as he went away on his sliding black feet. He should have a good tip when they left — a pound note at least.

The muezzin was still calling. It seemed an hour since he had begun. Returning to the bathroom, Chapman stood in the french doors looking out at the town. In the gray light the palm tops lay as quiet as something under glass. The yellow paths of the back garden were quiet geometry below him, and he smelled the authentic, wet-mud smell of Egypt. Across wall and roofs was a yellow reach of river, with a narrow mud island lying against the far shore, then a strip of taffy-colored water, then the shore itself and the far lines of palms indicating villages or canals, and clear beyond, binding the edge of the pure sky, the long desert rim that divided habitable Egypt from the wastes.

Over there was the City of the Dead, where the light had been last night and where he had half imagined ghouls and vampires, jackal-headed men with square shoulders, ob-scene prowling things. It was innocent and clean now, and the river that when they first came had seemed to him a dirty, mud-banked sewer looked different too. It came down grandly, one of the really mighty rivers, pouring not

so much out of the heart of the continent as out of all backward time, and in its yellow water it carried the rich silt for
delta cotton fields, the bilharzia worms to infect the sweating fellahin at the ditch heads, the sewage and the waste,
the fecundity, the feculence. The river was literally Egypt.
Lotus and papyrus, ibis and crocodile, there it came. In-
comprehensibly, tears jumped to his eyes. He went into
the bedroom and got the binoculars and returned to watch.

The blurry yellow haze sharpened into precise lines as he
turned the knob. Beyond the mud margins he saw a line of
people coming, leading donkeys and camels loaded with
something, perhaps produce for the market. He saw them
carry burdens from beast to boat. Farther down, a family
was bathing in the river, a woman and four children, who
ran and splashed each other and launched themselves like
sleds on the water. The thought of swimming in that open
drain appalled him — and yet why not? Probably it never
occurred to them that the river was polluted. And it was a
touching and private thing, somehow, to see the brown-
skinned family playing and see them so close and unaware
and yet not hear their shouting and laughter.

The far bank was fully alive now. Two feluccas were
slanting out across the current of the river, and the river
seemed not so much to divide as to unite its two shores.
Birds flew over it, camels and donkeys and people clustered
at the landing places, the feluccas moved, leaning farther in
a riffle of wind. All the Nile's creatures, as inexhaustible as
the creatures of the sea, began to creep and crawl and fly.
Safe, relieved of anxiety, reassured, rescued, Chapman
watched them from his little cell of sanitary plumbing, and
on his hands as he held the binoculars to his eyes he
smelled the persistent odor of antiseptic.

It was ridiculous, but they made him feel alone and

timid. He wished his son would awake so they could talk.
He could read aloud to him during the time he was getting
stronger; the thought occurred to him as an opportunity he
must not miss.

"What a damned country!" he said.

Watching the river, he had not noticed the movement at
the far corner of the garden below him, but now as he
swung the glasses down he saw there one of the ragged,
black-robed boys who raked and sprinkled the paths every
day. He had taken off his turban and was kneeling, folding
it back and forth until it made a little mat beside one of the
garden water taps. On this he knelt, and with a reaching
haul pulled the robe over his head. He wore nothing else.
His ribs were like the ribs of a basket, his shoulder blades
moved as he turned on the tap.

Steadying the glasses against the jamb, Chapman
watched the brown boy's face, very serious and composed,
and as it turned momentarily he thought he saw one milky
blind eye. Face, neck, shoulders, arms, chest and belly, and
carefully the loins and rectum, the boy washed himself with
cupped handfuls of water. He washed his feet one after
the other, he bent and let the tap run a moment over his
head. On the yellow ground a dark spot of wet grew.

He stood up, and Chapman stepped back, not to be
caught watching, but the boy only pulled on his robe again.
Then he knelt once more on the rug of his turban and
bowed himself in prayer toward the east.

Chapman kept the glasses steadily on him. The intense
concentration and stillness of the bent figure bothered him
obscurely. He remembered himself staring at the tiled wall
and did not like the memory. Moreover, the shame of that
evasion was mixed with an irritated, unwilling perception

that the boy kneeling in the garden was humble, touching, even dignified.

Dignified? A skinny, one-eyed boy with a horizon no wider than the garden he worked in, with one dirty robe to his back, and for home a mud hut where the pigeons nested in the living room and the buffalo owned the inner, safest, most desirable room? The image of Egyptian workmen he had seen picking up the dirt-caked hems of their robes and holding them in their teeth for greater freedom of action stood in his mind like stiff sculpture.

And yet the praying boy was not pathetic or repulsive or ridiculous. His every move was assured, completely natural. His touching of the earth with his forehead made Chapman want somehow to lay a hand on his bent back.

They have more death than we do, Chapman thought. Whatever he is praying to has more death in it than anything we know.

Maybe it had more life too. Suppose he had sent up a prayer of thanksgiving a little while ago when he found his son out of danger? He had been doing something like praying all night, praying to modern medicine, propitiating science, purifying himself with germicides, placating the germ theory of disease. But suppose he had prayed in thanksgiving, where would he have directed his prayer? Not to God, not to Allah, not to the Nile or any of its creature-gods or the deities of light. To some laboratory technician in a white coat. To the Antibiotic God. For the first time it occurred to him what the word antibiotic really meant.

The distant rim was light-struck now. The first of the morning buzzards came from somewhere and planed across the motionless palm tops. It teetered and banked close so that Chapman saw the curve of its head like the vulture-headed image on the boy's bed table: the vulture head of Mut, the Lady of Thebes, the Mother of the World. They eyed each other with a kind of recognition as it passed. It had a look like patience, and its shadow, passing and returning over the garden, brushing the ragged boy and the palms and the balcony where Chapman stood, might have seemed a threat but might also have been a kind of patrolling, almost a reassurance.

pop goes
the
alley cat

GETTING up to answer the door, Prescott looked into the face of a Negro boy of about eighteen. Rain pebbled his greased, straightened hair; the leather yoke of his blazer and the knees of his green gabardine pants were soaked. The big smile of greeting that had begun on his face passed over as a meaningless movement of the lips. "I was lookin'," he said, and then with finality, "I thought maybe Miss Vaughn."

"She's just on her way out."

The boy did not move. "I like to see her," he said, and gave Prescott a pair of small, opaque, expressionless eyes to look into. Eventually Prescott motioned him in. He made a show of getting the water off himself, squee-geeing his hair with a flat palm, shaking his limber hands, lifting the wet knees of his pants with thumb and finger as he sat down. He was not a prepossessing specimen: on the scrawny side, the clothes too flashy but not too clean, the mouth loose and always moving, the eyes the kind that shifted everywhere when you tried to hold them but were on you intently the moment you looked away.

But he made himself at home. And why not, Prescott asked himself, in this apartment banked and stacked and overflowing with reports on delinquency, disease, crime, discrimination; littered with sociological studies and affidavits on police brutality and the mimeographed communications of a dozen betterment organizations? The whole place was a temple to the juvenile delinquent, and here was the god himself in the flesh, Los Angeles Bronzeville model.

Well, he said, I am not hired to comment, but only to make pictures.

Carol came into the hall from her bedroom, and Prescott saw with surprise that she was glad to see this boy. "Johnny!" she said. "Where did you drop from?"

Over the boy had come an elaborate self-conscious casualness. He walked his daddylonglegs fingers along the couch back and lounged to his feet, rolling the collar of the blazer smooth across the back of his neck. Prescott was reminded of the slickers of his high school days, with their pinch-waisted bell-bottomed suits and their habit of walking a little hollow-chested to make their shoulders look wider. The boy weaved and leaned, pitching his voice high for kidding, moving his shoulders, his mouth, his pink-palmed hands. "Start to rain on me," he said in the high complaining humorous voice. "Water start comin' down on me I think I have to drop in."

"How come you're not working?"

"That job!" the boy said, and batted it away with both hands. "That wasn't much of a job, no kiddin'."

"Wasn't?"

"You know. Them old flour bags heavy, you get tired. Minute you stop to rest, here come that old foreman with

the *gooseroo*. Hurry up there, boy! Get along there, boy!
They don't ride white boys like that."

Carol gave Prescott the merest drawing down of the lips.
"That's the third job in a month," she said, and added,
"Johnny's one of my boys. Johnny Bane. This is Charlie
Prescott, Johnny."

"Pleased to meet you," Johnny said without looking.
Prescott nodded and withdrew himself, staring out into
the dripping garden court.

"You know a fact?" Johnny said. "That old strawboss
keep eyeballin' me and givin' me that old hurry-up, hurry-
up, that gets *old*. I get to carryin' my knife up the sleeve
of my sweatshirt, and he comes after me once *more*, I'm
goin' *cut* him. So I quit before I get in bad trouble out
there."

Carol laughed, shaking her head. "At least that's ingen-
ious. What'll you do now?"

"Well, I don't *know*." He wagged his busy hands. "No
future pushin' a truck around or cuttin' *lemons* off a tree. I
like me a job with some *class*, you know, something where
I could *learn* something."

"I can imagine how ambition eats away at you."

"No kiddin'!" the burbling voice said. "I get real in-
dustrious if I had me the right *kind* of a job. Over on
Second Street there's this Chinaman, he's on call out at
Paramount. Everytime they need a Chinaman for a mob
scene, out he goes and runs around for a couple of hours
and they hand him all this *lettuce*, man. You know anybody
out at MGM, Paramount, anywhere?"

"No," she said. "Do you, Charlie?"

"Nobody that needs any Chinamen." Prescott showed
her the face of his watch. Johnny Bane was taking in, apparently for the first time, the camera bag, the tripod, the

canvas sack of flash bulbs beside Prescott's chair.

"Hey, man, you a photographer?"

"Charlie and I are doing a picture study of your part of town for the Russell Foundation," Carol said.

"Take a long time to be a photographer?" Johnny's mouth still worked over his words, but now that his attention was fixed his eyes were as unblinking as an alligator's.

"Three or four years."

"Man, that's a rough *sentence!* Take a long time, uh? Down by the station there's this place, mug you for a quarter. Sailors and their chicks always goin' in. One chick I was watchin' other night, she had her picture five times. Lots of cats and chicks, every night. *Money* in that, man."

She shook her head, saying, "Johnny, when are you going to learn to hold a job? You make it tough for me, after I talk you into a place."

"I get me in trouble, I stay over there," he said. "I know you don't want me gettin' into trouble." Lounging, crossing his feet, he said, "I like to learn me some trade. Like this photography. I bet I surprise you. That ain't like pushin' a truck with some *foreman* givin' you the eyeballs all the time."

Prescott lifted the camera bag to the chair. "If we're going to get anything today we'll have to be moving."

"Just a minute," Carol said. To Johnny she said, "Do you know many people over on your hill?"

"Sure, man. *Multitudes.*"

"Mexicans too?"

"They're mostly Mexicans over there. My chick's Mexican." He staggered with his eyes dreamily shut. "Solid, solid!" he said.

"He might help us get in some places," Carol said. "What do you think, Charlie?"

Prescott shrugged.

"He could hold reflectors and learn a little about photography."

Prescott shrugged again.

"Do you mind, Charlie?"

"You're the doctor." He handed the sack of flash bulbs and the tripod to Johnny and picked up the camera bag. "Lesson number one," he said. "A photographer is half packhorse."

The *barrio* was a double row of shacks tipping from a hilltop down a steep road clayily shining and deserted in the rain, every shack half buried under climbing roses, geraniums, big drooping seedheads of sunflowers, pepper and banana trees, and palms: a rural slum of the better kind, the poverty overlaid deceptively with flowers. Across the staggering row of mailboxes Prescott could see far away, over two misty hilltops and an obscured sweep of city, the Los Angeles Civic Center shining a moment in a watery gleam of sun.

Johnny hustled around, pulling things from the car. As Prescott took the camera bag, the black face mugged and contorted itself with laughter. "You want me and my chick? How about me and my chick cuttin' a little *jive*, real mean? Colored and Mexican hobnobbin'. That okay?"

"First some less sizzling shots," Carol said dryly. "Privies in the rain, ten kids in a dirt-floored shack. How about Dago Aguirre's? That's pretty bad, isn't it?"

"Dago's? Man, that's a real *dump*. You want dumps, uh? Okay, we try Dago's."

He went ahead of them, looking back at the bag Prescott carried. "Must cost a lot of lettuce, man, all those *cameras*."

Prescott shook the bag at him. "That's a thousand dollars in my hand," he said. "That's why I carry it myself."

Rain had melted the adobe into an impossible stickiness; after ten steps their feet were balls of mud. Johnny took them along the flat hilltop to a gateless fence under a sugar palm, and as they scraped the mud from their shoes against a broken piece of concrete a Mexican boy in Air Force dungarees opened the door of the shack and leaned there.

"*Ese, Dago,*" Johnny said.

"*Hórale, cholo.*" Dago looked down without expression as Johnny shifted the tripod and made a mock-threatening motion with his fist.

"We came to see if we could take some pictures," Carol said. "Is your mother home, Dago?"

Dago oozed aside and made room for a peering woman with a child against her shoulder. She came forward uncertainly, a sweet-faced woman made stiff by mistrust. Carol talked to her in Spanish for five minutes before she would open her house to them.

Keeping his mouth shut and working fast as he had learned to on this job, Prescott got the baby crawling on the dirt floor between pans set to catch the drip from the roof. He got the woman and Dago and the baby and two smaller children eating around the table whose one leg was a propped box. By backing into the lean-to, between two old iron bedsteads, and having Carol, Johnny, and Dago hold flashes in separate corners, he got the whole place, an orthodox FSA shot, Standard Poverty. That was what the Foundation expected. As always, the children cried when the flashes went off; as always he mollified them with the blown bulbs, little Easter eggs of shellacked glass. It was a dump, but nothing out of the ordinary, and he got no picture that excited him until he caught the woman nursing her baby on a box in the corner. The whole story was there in the protective stoop of her figure and the drained resignation of her face. She looked anciently tired; the baby's chubby hand was clenched in the flesh of her breast.

Johnny Bane, eager beaver, brisk student, had been officious about keeping extension cords untangled and posing with the reflector. By the time Prescott had the camera and tripod packed Johnny had everything else dismantled. "How you get all them *lights* to go off at *once?*" he said.

Prescott dropped a reflector and they both stooped for it, bumping heads. The boy's skull felt as hard as cement; for a moment Prescott was unreasonably angry. But he caught Carol's eye across the room, and straightening up without a word he showed Johnny and Dago how the flashes were synchronized, he let them look into the screen of the Rolleiflex, he explained shutter and lens, he gave them a two-minute lecture on optics. "Okay?" he said to Carol in half-humorous challenge.

She smiled. "Okay."

The Aguirre family watched them to the door and out into the drizzle. Johnny Bane, full of importance, a hep cat, a photographer's assistant, punched the shoulder of the lounging Dago. "*Ay te wacho,*" he said. Dago lifted a languid hand.

"Now what?" Prescott asked.

"More of the same," Carol said. "Unfortunately, there's plenty."

"Overcrowding, malnutrition, lack of sanitation," he said. "Four days of gloom. Can't we shoot something pretty?"

"There's always Johnny's chick."

"Maybe she comes under the head of lack of sanitation."

They were all huddled under the sugar palm. "What

about my chick?" Johnny demanded. "You want my chick now?"

Carol stood tying a scarf over her fair hair. In raincoat and saddle shoes, she looked like a college sophomore. "Does your chick's family approve of you?" she said. "Most Mexican families aren't too happy to see boy friends hanging around."

Tickled almost to idiocy, he cackled and flapped his hands. "Man, they think I'm *rat* poison, no kiddin'. They think *any* cat's rat poison. They got this old Mexican jive about keepin' chicks at *home*. But I come there with you, they got to let me *in*, don't they?"

"So who's helping whom?" Prescott said.

That made him giggle and mug all the way down the slippery hill. "Hey, man," he said once, "you know these Mexicans believe in this Evil Eye, this *ojo*. When I hold up that old reflector I'm sayin' the Lord's Prayer backwards and puttin' the eyeballs on him, and when here comes that big flash, man, her old man really think he got the curse on him. I tell him I don't take it off till he let Lupe go out any time she want. Down to that *beach*, man. She look real mean down there on that sand gettin' the eyeballs from all the cats. *Reety!*"

"Spare us the details," Carol said, and turned her face from the rain, hanging to a broken fence and slipping, laughing, coming up hard against a light pole. Prescott slithered after her until before a shack more pretentious than most, almost a cottage, Johnny kicked the mud from his shoes and silently mugged at them, with a glassy, scared look in his odd little eyes, before he knocked on the home-made door.

It was like coming into a quiet opening in the woods and startling all the little animals. They were watched by a dozen pairs of eyes. Prescott looked past the undershirted Mexican who had opened the door and saw three men with cards and glasses and a jug before them on a round table. A very pregnant woman stood startled in the middle of the floor. On a bed against the far wall a boy had lowered his comic book to stare. There was a flash of children disappearing into corners and behind the stove. The undershirted man welcomed them with an enveloping winy breath but his smile was only for Carol and Prescott; his recognition of Johnny was a brief, sidelong lapse from politeness. Somewhere behind the door a phonograph was playing "Linda Mujer"; now it stopped with a squawk.

Once, during the rapid Spanish that went on between Carol and the Mexican, Prescott glanced at Johnny, but the boy's face, with an unreal smile pasted on it, blinked and peered past the undershirted man as if looking for someone. His forehead was puckered in tense knots. Then the undershirted man said something over his shoulder, the men at the table laughed, and one lifted the jug in invitation. The host brought it and offered it to Carol, who grinned and tipped and drank while they applauded. Then Prescott, mentally tasting the garlic and chile from the lips that had drunk before him, coldly contemplating typhoid, diphtheria, polio, drank politely and put the jug back in the man's hands with thanks and watched him return it to the table without offering it to Johnny Bane. They were pulled into the room, the door closed, and he saw that the old hand-cranked Victrola had been played by a Mexican youth in drape pants and a pretty girl, short-skirted and pompadoured. The girl should be Lupe, Johnny's chick. He looked for the glance of understanding between them and saw only the look on Johnny's face as if he had an unbearable belly ache.

This was a merry shackful. The men were all a little drunk, and posed magnificently and badly, their eyes magnetized by the camera. The boy was lured from his comic book. Lupe and the youth, who turned out to be her cousin Chuey, leaned back and watched and whispered with a flash of white teeth. As for Johnny, he held reflectors where Prescott told him to, but he was no longer an eager beaver. His mouth hung sullenly; his eyes kept straying to the two on the couch.

Dutifully Prescott went on with his job, documenting poverty for humanitarianism's sake and humanizing it as he could for the sake of art. He got a fair shot of the boy reading his comic book under a hanging image of the Virgin, another of two little girls peeking into a steaming kettle of frijoles while the mother modestly hid her pregnancy behind the stove. He shot the card players from a low angle, with low side-lighting, and when an old grandmother came in the back door with a pail of water he got her there, stooping to the weight in the open door, against the background of the rain.

Finally he said into Carol's ear, with deliberate malice, "Now do we get that red-hot shot of Johnny jiving with his chick?"

"You're a mean man, Charlie," she said, but she smiled, and looking across to where Johnny stood sullen and alone she said, "Johnny, you want to come over here?"

He came stiff as a stick, ugly with venom and vanity. When Carol seated him close to Lupe the girl rolled her eyes and bit her lip, ready to laugh. The noise in the room had quieted; it was as if a dipperful of cold water had been thrown into a boiling kettle. Carol moved Chuey in close and laid some records in Lupe's lap. Prescott could see the caption coming up: *Even in shacktown, young people need* amusement. Lack of adequate entertainment facilities one of greatest needs. Older generation generally disapproves of jive, jive talk, jive clothes.

The girl was pretty, even with her ridiculous pompadour. Her eyes were soft, liquid, very dark, her cheekbones high, and her cheeks planed. With a *rebozo* over her head she might have posed for Murillo's Madonna. She did not stare into the camera as her elders did, but at Prescott's word became absorbed in studying the record labels. Chuey laid his head close to hers, and on urging, Johnny sullenly did the same. The moment the flash went off Johnny stood up.

Prescott shifted the Victrola so the crank handle showed more, placed Chuey beside it with a record in his hands. "All right, Lupe, you and Johnny show us a little rug-cutting."

He watched the girl glance from the corners of her eyes at her parents, then come into Johnny's arm. He held her as if she smelled bad, his head back and away, but she turned her face dreamily upward and sighed like an actress in a love drama and laid her face against his rain-wet chest. "*Que chicloso!*" she said, and could not hold back her laughter.

"*Surote!*" Johnny pushed her away so hard she almost fell. His face was contorted, his eyes glared. Spittle sprayed from his heavy lips. "*Bofa!*" he said to Lupe, and suddenly Prescott found himself protecting the camera in the middle of what threatened to become a brawl. Chuey surged forward, the undershirted father crowded in from the other side, the girl was spitting like a cat. With a wrench Johnny broke away and got his back to the wall, and there he stood with his hand plunged into the pocket of his blazer and his loose mouth working.

"Please!" Carol was shouting, "Chuey! Lupe! Please!"

She held back the angry father and got a reluctant, broken quiet. Over her shoulder she said, "Johnny, go wait for us in the car."

For a moment he hung, then reached a long thin hand for the latch and slid out. The room was instantly full of noise again, indignation, threats. Prescott got his things safely outside the door away from their feet, and by that time politeness and diplomacy had triumphed. Carol said something to Lupe, who showed her teeth in a little white smile; to Chuey, who shrugged; to the father, who bowed over her hand and talked close to her face. There was hand-shaking around, Carol promised them prints of the pictures, Prescott gave the children each a quarter. Eventually they were out in the blessed rain.

"What in hell did he call her?" Prescott said as they clawed their way up the hill.

"Pachuco talk. Approximately a chippy."

"Count on him for the right touch."

"Don't say anything, Charlie," she said. "Let me handle him."

"He's probably gone off somewhere to nurse his wounded ego."

But as he helped her over the clay brink onto the cinder road he looked toward the car and saw the round dark head in the back seat. "I must say you pick some dillies," he said.

Walking with her face sideward away from the rain, she said seriously, "I don't pick them, Charlie. They come because they don't have anybody else."

"It's no wonder this one hasn't got anybody else," he said, and then they were at the car and he was opening the door to put the equipment inside. Johnny Bane made no motion to get his muddy feet out of the road.

"Lunch?" Carol said as she climbed under the wheel. Prescott nodded, but Johnny said nothing. In the enclosed car Prescott could smell his hair oil. Carol twisted around to smile at him.

"Listen!" she said. "Why take it so hard? It's just that Chuey's her cousin, he's family, he can crash the gate."

"Agh!"

"Laugh it off."

He let his somber gaze fall on her. "That punk!" he said. "I get him good. Her too. I kill that mean little bitch. You wait. I kill her sometime."

For a moment she watched him steadily; then she sighed. "If it helps to take it out on me, go ahead," she said. "I'll worry about you, if that's what you want."

A few minutes later she stopped at a diner on Figueroa, but when she and Prescott climbed out, Johnny sat still. "Coming?" she said.

"I ain't hungry."

"Oh, Johnny, come off it! Don't sulk all day."

The long look he gave her was so deliberately insolent that Prescott wanted to reach through the window and slap his loose mouth. Then the boy looked away, picked a thread indifferently from his sleeve, stared moodily as if tasting some overripe self-pity or some rich revenge. Prescott took Carol's arm and pulled her into the diner.

"Quite a young man," he said.

Her look was sober. "Don't be too hard on him."

"Why not?"

"Because everybody always has been."

He passed her the menu. "Mother loved me, but she died."

"Stop it, Charlie!"

He was astonished. "All right," he said at last. "Forget it."

While they were eating dessert she ordered two hamburgers to go, and when she passed them through the car window Johnny Bane took them without a word. "What do you want to do?" she said. "Come along, or have us drop you somewhere?"

"Okay if I go along?"

"Sure."

"Okay."

In a street to which she drove, a peddler pushed a cart full of peppers and small Mexican bananas through the mud between dingy frame buildings. No one else was on the street, but two children were climbing through the windows of a half-burned house. The rain angled across, fine as mist.

"What's here?" Prescott said.

"This is a family I've known ever since I worked for Welfare," Carol said. "Grandmother with asthma, father with dropsy, half a dozen little rickety kids. This is to prove that bad luck has no sense of proportion."

Fishing for a cigarette, Prescott found the package empty. He tried the pockets of coat and raincoat without success. Carol opened her purse; she too was out. Johnny Bane had been smoking hers all morning.

"We can find a store," she said, and had turned the ignition key to start when Johnny said, "I can go get some for you."

"Oh, say, would you, Johnny? That would be wonderful."

Prescott felt dourly that he was getting an education in social workers. One rule was that the moment your delinquent showed the slightest sign of decency, passed you a cigarette or picked up something you had dropped, you fell on his neck as if he had rescued you from drowning. As a matter of fact, he had felt his own insides twitch with surprised pleasure at Johnny's offer. But then what? he asked himself. After you've convinced him that every little decency of his deserves a hundred times its weight in thanks, then what?

"No stores around here," Johnny said. "Probably the nearest over on Figueroa."

"Oh," she said, disappointed. "Then I guess we'd better drive down. That's too far to walk."

"You go ahead, do your business here," Johnny said. He leaned forward with his hands on the back of the front seat. "I take the car and go get some weeds, how's that?"

Prescott waited to hear what she would say, but he really knew. After a pause her quiet voice said, "Have you got a driver's license?"

"Sure, man, right here."

"All right," she said, and stepped out. "Don't be long. Charlie dies by inches without smokes."

While Prescott unloaded, Johnny slid under the wheel. He was as jumpy as a greyhound. His fingers wrapped around the wheel with love.

"Wait," Carol said. "I didn't give you any money."

With an exclamation Prescott fished a dollar bill from his pocket and threw it into the seat, and Johnny Bane let off the emergency and rolled away.

"What was that?" Prescott said. "Practical sociology?"

"Don't be so indignant," she said. "You trust people, and maybe that teaches them to trust you."

"Why should anybody but a hooligan have to be *taught* to trust you? Are you so unreliable?"

But she only shook her head at him, smiling and denying his premises, as they went up the rotted steps.

This house was worse than the others. It was not merely poor, it was dirty, and it was not merely dirty, but sick. Prescott looked it over for picture possibilities while Carol talked with a thin Mexican woman, worn to the bleak collarbones, with arms like sticks. In the kitchen the sink was stopped with a greasy rag, and dishes swam in water the color of burlap. On the table were three bowls with brown juice dried in them. There was a hole clear through the kitchen wall. In the front room, on an old taupe overstuffed sofa, the head of the house lay in a blanket bathrobe, his thickened legs exposed, his eyes mere slits in the swollen flesh of his face. By the window in the third room an old woman sat in an armchair, and everywhere, in every corner and behind every broken piece of furniture, were staring broad-faced children, incredibly dirty and as shy as mice. In a momentary pause in Carol's talk he heard the native sounds of this house: the shuffle of children's bare feet and the old woman's harsh breathing.

He felt awkward, and an intruder. Imprisoned by the rain, quelled by the presence of the Welfare lady and the strange man, the children crept soft as lizards around the walls. Wanting a cigarette worse than ever, Prescott glanced impatiently at his watch. Probably Johnny would stop for a malt or drive around showing off the car and come in after an hour expecting showers of thanks.

"What do you think, Charlie?" Carol's voice had dropped; the bare walls echoed to any noise, the creeping children and the silent invalids demanded hushed voices and soft feet. "Portrait shots?" she whispered. "All this hopeless sickness?"

"They'll be heartbreakers."

"That's what they ought to be."

Even when he moved her chair so that gray daylight fell across her face, the old woman paid no attention to him beyond a first piercing look. Her head was held stiffly, her face as still as wood, but at every breath the cords in her neck moved slightly with the effort. He got three time exposures of that half-raised weathered mask: flash would have destroyed what the gray light revealed.

Straightening up from the third one, he looked through the doorway into the inhuman swollen face of the son. It was impossible to tell whether the Chinese slits of eyes were looking at him or not. He was startled with the thought that they might be, and wished again, irritably, for a cigarette.

"Our friend is taking his time," he said to Carol, and held up his watch.

"Maybe he couldn't find a store."

Prescott grunted, staring at the dropsical man. If he shot across the swollen feet and legs, foreshortening them, and into the swollen face, he might get something monstrous and sickening, a picture to make people wince.

"Can he be propped up a little?" he asked.

Carol asked the thin, hovering wife, who said he could. The three of them lifted and slid the man up until his shoulders were against the wall. It troubled Prescott to see Carol's hands touch the repulsive flesh. The man's slits watched them, the lips moved, mumbling something.

"What's he say?"

"He says you must be a lover of beauty," Carol said.

For a moment her eyes held his, demanding of him something that he hated to give. Once, on his only trip to

Mexico, he had gone hunting with his host in Michoacan, and he remembered how he had fired at a noise in a tree and brought something crashing down, and how they had run up to see a little monkey lying on the bloodied leaves. It was still alive; as they came up its eyes followed them, and at a certain moment it put up its arms over its head to ward off the expected death blow. To hear this monster make a joke was like seeing that monkey put up its arms in an utterly human gesture. It sickened him so that he took refuge behind the impersonality of the camera, and when he had taken his pictures he said something that he had not said to a subject all day. "Thanks," he said. "Gracias, señor."

Somehow he had to counteract that horrible portrait with something sweet. He posed the thin mother and one of the children in a sentimental Madonna and Child pose, pure poster art suitable for a fund-raising campaign. While he was rechecking for the second exposure he heard the noise, like a branch being dragged across gravel. It came from the grandmother. She sat in the same position by the window of the other room, but she seemed straighter and more rigid, and he had an odd impression that she had grown in size.

The thin woman was glancing uneasily from Prescott to Carol. The moment he stepped back she was out of her chair and into the other room.

The grandmother had definitely grown in size. Prescott watched her with a wild feeling that anyone in this house might suddenly blow up with the obscene swelling disease. Under the shawl the old woman's chest rose in jerky breaths, but it didn't go down between inhalations. Her gray face shone with sudden sweat; her mouth was open, her head held stiffly to one side.

"Hadn't I better try to get a doctor?" Prescott said.

Bending over the old woman, Carol turned only enough to nod.

Prescott went quickly to the door. The peddler had disappeared, the children who had been climbing in the burned house were gone, the street lay empty in the rain. Johnny Bane had been gone for over an hour; if this woman died he could take the credit. In a district like this there might not be a telephone for blocks. Prescott would have to run foolishly like someone shouting fire.

A girl of ten or so, sucking her thumb, slid along the wall, watching him. He trapped her. "Where's there a telephone?"

She stared, round-eyed and scared.

"*Telefono? You sabe telefono?*"

He saw comprehension grow in her face, slapped a half-dollar into her hand, motioned her to start leading him. She went down the steps and along the broken sidewalk at a trot.

It took four calls from the little neighborhood grocery before he located a doctor who could come. Then, the worst cause for haste removed, he paused to buy cigarettes for himself and a bag of suckers for the children. His guide put a sucker in her mouth and a hand in his, and they walked back that way through the drizzle.

The street before the house was still empty, and he cursed Johnny Bane. Inside, the grandmother was resting after her paroxysm, but her head was still stiffly tilted, and a minute after he entered she fell into a fit of coughing that pebbled her lips with mucus and brought her halfway to her feet, straining and struggling for air. Carol and the thin woman held her, eased her back.

"Did you get someone?" Carol said.

"He's on his way."

"Did he tell you anything to do?"

"There's nothing to do except inject atropine or something. We have to wait for him."

"Hasn't Johnny come back?"

"Did you really expect him to?"

Her eyes and mouth were strained. She no longer looked like a college sophomore: a film from the day's poverty and sickness had rubbed off on her. Without a word she turned away, went into the kitchen, and started clearing out the sink.

As Prescott started to pack up it occurred to him that a picture of an old woman choking to death would add to the sociological impact of Carol's series, but he was damned if he would take it. He'd had enough for one day. The dropsical man turned his appalling swollen mask, and on an impulse Prescott stood up and gestured with the pack of cigarettes. The monster nodded, so Prescott inserted a cigarette between the lips and lighted it. Sight of the man smoking fascinated him.

The Rolleiflex was just going into the bag when it struck him that he had not seen the Contax. He rummaged, turned things out onto the floor. The camera was gone. Squatting on his heels, he considered how he should approach the mother of the house, or Carol, to get it back from whichever child had taken it. And then he began to wonder if it had been there when he unpacked for this job. He had used it at the Aguirre house for one picture, but not since. The bag had been in the car all the time he and Carol had been eating lunch. So had Johnny Bane.

Carefully refusing to have any feeling at all about the matter, he took his equipment out on the porch. Four or five children, each with a sucker in its mouth, came out and shyly watched him as he smoked and waited for the doctor.

The doctor was a short man with an air of unhurried haste. He examined the grandmother for perhaps a minute and got out a needle. The woman's eyes followed his hands with terror as he swabbed with an alcohol-soaked pad, jabbed, pushed with his thumb, withdrew, dropped needle and syringe into his case. It was like an act of deadpan voodoo. Within minutes the old woman was breathing almost normally, as if the needle had punctured her swelling and let her subside. For a minute more the doctor talked with Carol; he scribbled on a pad. Then his eyes darted into the next room to where the swollen son lay watching from his slits.

"What's the matter in here?"

"Dropsy," Carol said. "He's been bedridden for months."

"Dropsy's a symptom, not a disease," the doctor said, and went over.

In ten more minutes they were all out on the porch again. "I'll expect you to call me then," the doctor said.

"I will," Carol said. "You bet I will."

"Are you on foot? Can I take you anywhere?"

"No thanks. We're just waiting for my car."

It was then four-thirty. Incredulously Prescott watched her sit down on the steps to wait some more. The late sun, scattering the mist, touched her fair hair and deepened the lines around her mouth. Behind her the children moved softly. Above her head the old porch pillar was carved with initials and monikers: GJG, Mingo, Lola, Chavo, Pina, Juanito. A generation of lost kids had defaced even the little they had, as they might deface and abuse anyone who tried to help them in ways too unselfish for them to understand.

"How long do you expect to sit here?" he said finally.

"Give him another half hour."

"He could have gone to Riverside for cigarettes and been back by now."

"I know."

"You know he isn't going to come back until he's brought."

"He was upset about his girl," she said. "He felt he'd been kicked in the face. Maybe he went up there."

"To do what? Cut her throat?"

"It isn't impossible," she said, and turned her eyes up to his with so much anxiety in them that he hesitated a moment before he told her the rest.

"Maybe it isn't," he said then, "but I imagine he went first of all to a pawnshop to get rid of the camera."

"Camera?"

"He swiped the Contax while we were having lunch."

"How do you know?"

"Either that or one of the kids here took it."

Her head remained bent down; she pulled a sliver from the step. "It couldn't have been here. I was here all the time. None of the children went near your stuff."

She knew so surely what Johnny Bane was capable of, and yet she let it trouble her so, that he was abruptly furious with her. Social betterment, sure, opportunities, yes, a helping hand, naturally. But to lie down and let a goon like that walk all over you, abuse your confidence, lie and cheat and steal and take advantage of every unselfish gesture!

"Listen," he said. "Let me give you a life history. We

turn him in and he comes back in handcuffs. Okay. That's six months in forestry camp, unless he's been there before."

"Once," she said, still looking down. "He was with a bunch that swiped a truck."

"Preston then," Prescott said. "In half a year he comes back from Preston and imposes on you some more, and you waste yourself keeping him out of trouble until he gets involved in something in spite of you, something worse, and gets put away for a stretch in San Quentin. By the time they let him out of there he'll be ripe for really big-time stuff, and after he's sponged on you for a while longer he'll shoot somebody in a holdup or knife somebody in a whorehouse brawl, and they'll lead him off to the gas chamber. And nothing you can do will keep one like him from going all the way."

"It doesn't have to happen that way. There's a chance it won't."

"It's a hell of a slim chance."

"I know it," she said, and looked up again, her face not tearful or sentimental as he had thought it would be, but simply thoughtful. "Slim or not, we have to give it to him."

"You've already given him ten chances."

"Even then," she said. "He's everything you say — he's mean, vicious, dishonest, boastful, vain, maybe dangerous. I don't like him any better than you do, any better than he likes himself. But he's told me things I don't think he ever told anyone else."

"He never had such a soft touch," he said.

"He grew up in a slum, Harlem. Routine case. His father disappeared before he was born, his mother worked, whatever she could find. He took care of himself."

"I understand that," Prescott said. "He's a victim. He

isn't to blame for what his life made him. But he's still unfit to live with other people. He isn't safe. Nine out of ten, maybe, you can help, but not his kind. It's too bad, but he's past helping."

"He wasn't a gang kid," she said. "He's unattractive, don't you see, and mean. People don't like him, and never did. He tries to run with the neighborhood Mexican gang here, but you saw how Chuey and Dago and Lupe just tolerate him. He doesn't belong. He never did. So he prowled the alleys and dreamed up fancy revenges for people he hated, and played with stray cats."

Prescott moved impatiently, and the children slid promptly further along the wall. Carol was watching him as steadily as the children were.

"He told me how he ran errands to earn money for liver and fish to feed them. He wanted them to come to him and be *his* cats."

Prescott waited, knowing how the script ran but surprised that Carol, a hardened case worker, should have fallen for it.

"But they were all alley cats, as outcast as he was," she said. "He'd feed a cat for a week, but when he didn't have anything for it, it would shy away, or he'd grab it and get clawed. So he used to try to tie cats up when he caught them."

Prescott said nothing.

"But when a cat wouldn't let itself be petted, or when it fought the rope — and it always did — he'd swing it by the rope and break its neck," Carol said.

She stirred the litter in the step corner and a sow bug rolled into its ball and bounced down into the dirt. " 'I give them every chance, Miss Vaughn,' that's what he told me. 'I give them every chance and if they won't come and be my friend I pop their neck.' "

Cautiously Prescott moved the camera bag backward with his foot. He looked at the afternoon's grime in the creases of his hands. "That's a sad story," he said at last. "I mean it, it really is. But it only proves what I said, that he's too warped to run loose. He might try that neck-popping on some human being who wouldn't play his way — Lupe, for instance."

"Would you pop a cat's neck if it wouldn't come to you?" Carol said softly.

"Don't be silly."

"But you'd pop Johnny's."

They stared at each other in the rainy late afternoon.

Prescott told himself irrelevantly that he had not fallen in love with her on this job. Anyone who fell in love with her would have to share her with every stray in Greater Los Angeles. But he liked her and respected her and admired her; she was a fine human being. Only she carried it too far.

And yet he had no answer for her. "Good God," he said, "do you know what you're asking?"

"Yes," she said. "I know exactly. But I know you can't come with liver and fish heads six days a week and on the seventh come with a hangman's rope. You can't say, 'I gave him every chance' unless you really did."

The brief sun had disappeared again in the mist and smog. The street was muddy and gray before them. Behind them the thin woman came to the door and opened it, shooing the children in with an unexpected harsh snarl in her voice. Prescott felt disturbed and alien, out of his proper setting and out of his depth. But he still could find no answer for her. You could not come with liver and fish heads six days a week and with a hangman's knot on the seventh. You could not put limits on love — if love was what you chose to live by.

"All right," he said. "We don't call the cops, is that it?"

She smiled a crooked smile. "Let's try to get along without the police as long as we can."

The thin woman stood in the doorway and said goodbye and watched them down the steps, and the children pressing around her flanks watched too. Prescott waved, and the woman smiled and nodded in reply. But none of the children, solemnly staring, raised a hand. After a moment he was angry with himself for having expected them to.

maiden
in a
tower

The highway entering Salt Lake City from the west curves around the southern end of Great Salt Lake past Black Rock and its ratty beaches, swings north away from the spouting smoke of the smelter towns, veers toward the onion-shaped domes of the Saltair Pavilion, and straightens out eastward again on the speedway. Ahead, across the white flats, the city and its mountains are a mirage, or a mural: metropolitan towers, then houses and trees and channeled streets, and then the mountain wall.

Driving into that, Kimball Harris began to feel like the newsreel diver whom the reversed projector sucks feet first out of his splash. Perhaps fatigue from the hard day and a half across the desert explained both the miragelike look of the city and his own sense that he was being run backward toward the beginning of the reel. But the feeling grew as he bored townward along the straight road, the same road out which, as a high school boy, he had driven much too fast in a stripped-down Ford bug with screaming companions in the rumble seat. They must have driven back, too, but he remembered only the going out. To see the city head-on, like this, was strange to him.

Middle-aged, rather tired, but alert with the odd notion that he was returning both through distance and through time, he passed the airport and the fair grounds and slowed for the first streets of the city.

Twenty-five years had made little difference. The city had spread some, and he was surprised, after the desert, by the green luxuriance of the trees, but the streets were still a half-mile wide, and water still ran in the gutters. It was really a good town, clean, with a freshness about it that revived him. Circling the Brigham Young monument, he nodded gravely to the figure with the outstretched hand, and like a native returning he went though the light and turned around the button in the middle of the block and came back to park before the Utah Hotel, careful to park well out from the curb so as not to block the flowing gutter. They gave you a ticket for that. It tickled him that he had remembered.

The doorman collared his bag, a bellhop climbed in to take the car around to the garage. Still running pleasantly backward into the reel, he went into the unchanged lobby and registered, and was carried up the unchanged elevators to the kind of room he remembered, such a room as they used to take when they held fraternity parties in the hotel, back in Prohibition times. During those years he had been on a diet for ulcers, and couldn't drink, but he had retired religiously with the boys, gargled raw Green River redeye, and spit it out again in the washbowl, only for the pleasure of lawbreaking and of carrying a distinguished breath back to the ballroom and the girls.

He shook his head, touched for a moment with his giddy and forgotten youth.

Later, fresh from the shower, with a towel around him, he picked up the telephone book, so dinky and provincial-seeming after the ponderous San Francisco directory that he caught himself feeling protective about it. But when he found the Merrill Funeral Parlors in the yellow pages he sat thinking, struck by the address: 363 East South Temple. On the Avenues side, just below Fourth East. He tried to visualize that once familiar street but it was all gone except for a general picture of tall stone and brick houses with high porches and lawns overtaken by plantain weeds. One, the one Holly had lived in, had a three-story stone tower.

That tower! With all the Jazz Age Bohemians crawling in and out. Havelock Ellis, Freud, Mencken, *The Memoirs of Fanny Hill*, *Love's Coming of Age*, *The Well of Loneliness*, Harry Kemp, Frank Harris. My Lord.

He was flooded with delighted recollection, they were all before him: reed-necked aesthetes, provincial cognoscenti, sad sexy yokels, lovers burning with a hard gemlike flame, a homosexual or two trying to look blasted and corroded by inward sin. Painters of bile-green landscapes, cubist photographers, poets and iconoclasts, scorners of the bourgeoisie, makers of cherished prose, dream-tellers, correspondence school psychoanalysts, they had swarmed through Holly's apartment and eddied around her queenly shape with noises like breaking china. He remembered her in her gold gown, a Proserpine or a Circe. For an instant she was slim and tall in his mind and he saw her laughing in the midst of the excitement she created, and how her hair was smooth black and her eyes very dark blue and how she wore massive gold hoops in her ears.

He wrote the number down and tucked it in the pocket of the suit laid out on the bed. But when he had dressed and gone down and was walking up South Temple past

Beehive House, Lion House, Eagle Gate, the old and new apartment buildings, he began to look at numbers with a feeling that approached suspense, and he searched not so much for the Merrill Funeral Parlors as for the house with the round stone tower. Finally he saw it, lifting across the roof of a mansion gone to seed, and in another thirty paces he could see the sign and the new brass numbers on the riser of the top porch step. It was the very house.

Quickly he looked around for landmarks to restore and brace his memory. Some of the old maples and hickories he remembered along the sidewalk were gone, the terrace rolled down with an unfamiliar smooth nap of grass. The porch no longer carried its sagging swing, and porch and steps had been renewed and painted. The door was as he remembered it, with lozenges of colored glass above it, and the doorknob's massive handful was an almost startling familiarity. But inside all was changed. Partitions had been gutted out. The stairs now mounted, or levitated, a spiral of white spokes and mahogany rails, from an expanse of plum-colored carpet. Instead of the cupping old parquetry his feet found softness, hushedness. The smells were of paint and flowers.

He was eying the stairs when a young man came out of an office on the left and bent his head a little leftward and said softly and pleasantly, "Yes, sir. Can I help?"

Harris brought himself dryly back to what he had driven eight hundred miles to do. He said, "I'm Kimball Harris. My aunt, Mrs. George Webb, died day before yesterday at the Julia Hicks Home. They telephoned me she would be here."

"We've been expecting you," the young man said, and put out his hand. "My name is McBride." A brief handshake, a moment when the young man regarded Harris with his head tilted. "Did you fly in?" he asked.

"Drove."

"All the way from San Francisco?"

"I slept a few hours in Elko."

"It wasn't so bad, then."

"Oh, no," Harris said. "Not bad at all."

In his mind was a faint amusement: this young man might have been left over from one of Holly's parties. He looked better equipped to write fragile verses than deal with corpses.

"She's in the parlor just back here," McBride said. "Would you like to see her? She looks very nice."

That would be young McBride's function, of course. He would be the one who made them look nice. "Maybe later," Harris said. "I expect there are some details we ought to settle."

"Of course," McBride said. "If you'll just step in here. We can look at caskets after a minute. You have a family cemetery plot, I believe? It will only take a minute for this. The details you can leave to us." He held the door wide, standing gracefully and deferentially back, and ushered Harris through.

A very few minutes seemed to settle the details. They rose, facing each other across the desk coolly glimmering in muted afternoon light. "Now would you like to see her?" McBride said.

Why, he takes pride, Harris thought. He probably stands back estimating his effects like a window dresser. Mister McBride, the Mortuary Max Factor. "All right," he said, "though it's not as if I had any tears to shed. I haven't seen her for twenty-five years, and she's been senile for ten."

McBride guided him around the unfamiliar stairs to

where the plum carpet flowed smoothly into what had evidently once been a dining room. "She does look nice," he said. "Very sweet and peaceful."

Which is more than she did alive, Harris thought, and went forward to the table with the basket of chrysanthemums at its foot. To remind himself that this was his mother's sister, his last near relative, made him feel nothing. Not even a deliberate attempt to squeeze sentimental recollections out of the past and remember suppers at Aunt Margaret's, Christmas visits at Aunt Margaret's, times when Aunt Margaret had unexpectedly given him a quarter, made the wax figure any dearer or realer. His indifference was so marked that he separated it and noticed it, wondering with a tinge of shame if he was callous. He supposed that if he had been attached to the dead woman he might think her peaceful, touching, even terrible. All he could think as he looked at her was that she looked well-embalmed — but then she had probably been close to mummified before she died.

Old Aunt Margaret, never very lovable, never dear to him in his childhood, and in his maturity only a duty and an expense, thrust her sharp nose, sharp cheekbones, withered lips, up through the rouge and lipstick and was, if she was not a total stranger, only old Aunt Margaret, mercifully dead at eighty-three. Harris did not even feel the conventional disgust with young McBride, who tampered with the dead. Considering what he had had to work with, McBride had done reasonably well.

Back in the hall again, he stood looking up the spiral stairs, apparently as unsupported as the Beanstalk, and remembered a time when Holly and three roommates — which three didn't matter, they changed so fast — came down the shabby old steps arguing about the proportions of the perfect female figure, and he met them on the second landing and like a chorus line they raised their skirts and thrust out their right legs before him, clamoring to know which was the most shapely. An undergraduate Paris and four demanding goddesses. He had picked Holly: why would he not?

McBride was in the office doorway. "We've just redone the whole place," he said. "It was the home of a Park City silver king originally, but it was all run down."

Harris was still looking up the stairs. McBride's words were no more important than the decorative changes, but upstairs there was something that was important, that pulled at him like an upward draft.

"I used to know this house twenty-five years ago," he said. "Some people I knew had an apartment on the third floor."

"Really? The front one or the back?"

"Front. The one with the round tower window."

"Oh yes," said McBride. "We haven't done much to that yet — just painted it."

"I wonder," Harris said, and made a little shrugging deprecatory motion and felt irritably ashamed, like a middle-aged man recalling last night's revels and his own unseemly capers and his pawing of the host's wife. It was fatuous to want to go up there, yet he did.

"Go on up if you want," McBride said. "The only thing, there's a woman laid out there."

"Well, then . . ."

"That wouldn't matter, if you don't mind. She's . . . presentable."

For a moment Harris hung on the word, and on the

thought that McBride's professional vanity was one of the odder kinds, and on a little fit of irritability that a corpse should intrude upon a sentimental but perfectly legitimate impulse. Then he put his hand on the mahogany rail. "Maybe I will."

The second-floor hall, at whose doors he had knocked or entered, was as much changed as the ground floor, but up the second flight of stairs he mounted into a growing familiarity. And he climbed against the pressure of a crowd of ghosts. The carpet ended at the stairhead; he put his feet down softly and held back his breath with the wild notion that he heard voices from the door of Holly's old apartment. Up these stairs, a hundred, two hundred, three hundred times, through how long? a year? two years? he had come with books or bottles or manuscripts in his hands and (it seemed to him now) an incomparable capacity for enthusiasm in his heart. From the high burlap-hung windows of the apartment inside they had let their liquid ridicule fall on the streets of the bourgeois city. He half expected, as he moved into the doorway, to see their faces look up inquiringly from chair and couch and floor.

But in the room there was only the dead woman, and she was not looking at him.

She lay on a wheeled table, with beside her one stiff chair and a taboret bearing a bowl of flowers, all of it composed as if for a macabre still life. Looking toward the window across the woman's body he saw how the gray light of afternoon blurred in her carefully-waved hair.

For a minute or two, perhaps, he stood in the doorway, stopped partly by the body and partly by the feeling of an obscure threat: he must summon and gather and recreate his recollections of this room; he was walking in a strange neighborhood and needed his own gang around him.

In Holly's time the tower bay had held an old upright piano, its backside exposed to the room like the hanging seat of a child's sleepers. Afternoons, evenings, Sunday and holiday mornings, there had been loud four-hand renderings of "Twelfth Street Rag," "St. Louis Blues," "Mood Indigo." On at least one Christmas morning they had even sung carols around it, syncopating them wickedly. That was the morning when he brought Holly the facsimile copy of The Marriage of Heaven and Hell — a mutinous book full of mottoes for their personalities and their times.

But what he remembered now, hanging in the doorway, was how in some lull in the bedlam that always went on there they had found themselves smiling foolishly at each other by the piano and she had put up her hands to his face and kissed him sweet and soft, a kiss like a happy child's. He realized now that he had recalled that kiss before, waking or sleeping, and that the memory of it had acquired a kind of caption, a fragment of the world's wisdom contributed to his adolescent store by a returned Mormon missionary: "Das ewig Weibliche zieht uns hinan," that remembered moment said.

How they had flocked and gathered there, debated, kissed, lied, shocked and astonished and delighted each other, there in the tower with Holly at their center, there by the vanished piano: poets and athletes, Renaissance heroes, fearless Stoics and impassioned Epicureans and abandoned Hedonists, girls with the bloom on their loveliness, goddesses with Perfect Proportions, artists and iconoclasts, as delighted with their own wickedness as if it had meant something.

He felt the stairs in his legs, the years in his mind, as he went in softly past the woman who lay so quietly on her back, and when he had passed her he turned and searched her face, almost as if he might surprise in it some expression meaningful to this wry and confusing return.

She was a plain woman, perhaps fifty. McBride had not yet made her look nice with rouge and lipstick. She lay in a simple black dress, but she had a Navajo squash-blossom necklace around her throat. It struck him as a remarkable piece of realism — perhaps something she had especially liked and had stubbornly worn even past the age when costume jewelry became her. It gave her a touching, naïvely rakish air.

Yet she shed a chill around her, and her silence spread to fill the room. Hardly a sound came through the stone walls. In the old days there had always been the piano banging, the phonograph going, two or six or sixteen voices making cosmic conversation. And he never remembered daylight in the apartment. Holly had affected a romantic gloom; the windows were always shrouded by the artistically-frayed burlap, and the light was from lamps, most of them low on the floor and some of them at least with red globes in them. And always the smell of sandalwood.

Like a Chinese whorehouse. He shook his head, pitying and entranced, and sat down on the window seat overlooking the reach of South Temple. Directly across was a Five Minute Car Wash with a big apron of concrete and a spick dazzle of white paint and red tiles. In the times he remembered, that lot had held a Peewee Golf Course where men in shirt sleeves, women in summer dresses, young couples loud with laughter, putted little white balls along precise green alleys and across precise circles of green artificial grass and over gentle and predictable bridges and causeways into numbered holes.

"Look at them," Holly said to him once as they sat in the tower looking down at the afterdinner golfers moving under the bright floodlights. "*Toujours gai*, my God. Some day I'm going to build a miniature golf course with fairways six inches wide and rough all over the place. I'll fill the water holes with full-sized crocodiles and sow the sandtraps with sidewinders. How would it be to hide a black widow spider in every hole so that holing out and picking up your ball would earn you some excitement? What if you sawed the supports of all the little bridges nearly in two?"

Live it dangerously. It was strange to recall how essential that had seemed. Go boom, take chances. He touched the casement windows, thinking that this was the pose, sitting right here and looking out, that Holly had assumed when Tom Stead painted her in her gold velvet gown.

Probably that portrait wasn't anything special. It couldn't have been. The chances were that Tom Stead was painting signs somewhere now, if he hadn't drunk himself to death. But then, in this room, in the presence of its subject whose life overflowed upon them all, that slim golden shape with the velvet highlights was Lilith, Helen, Guenevere, *das ewig Weibliche*. And it was hardly a day before other girls, less fortunately endowed or graced, had begun dropping comments on how *warm* that Stead-Holly romance was getting, and hinting that there was hidden away somewhere a companion portrait — a nude.

Well, well, what a bunch of Bohemian puritans. Harris did not believe in any nude, or in its importance if there had been one, though at the time it had bothered him, and he had been malely offended, surprised that she would *lower* herself, you know?

Now, sitting bemused in the window, he reflected that what had truly shone out of that golden portrait, as out of Holly herself, was not so much glamour as innocence.

Under the sheath she was positively virginal; if you cracked the enamel of her sophistication you found a delighted little girl playing Life.

Again he remembered the soft, childlike kiss by the piano on a Christmas morning, and he stood up so sharply that he startled himself with the sight of the dead woman. It was innocence. She could put away the predatory paws of college boys, twist laughing from the casual kiss, pass among the hot young Freudians as untouched as a nun, shed like water the propositions that were thrown at her seven to the week. There she sat in her gold gown by her window opening on the foam: a maiden in a tower.

He crossed the room and tried the bedroom door, wanting to look in on her intimately. In this room, now completely bare, aseptically painted, he had sat dozens of times when she was ill or when on Sunday mornings she made it a charming point of her sophistication to entertain in bed. While she lay propped with pillows he had read to her, talked to her, kissed her, had his hands fended away. The empty room was still charged with the vividness with which she invested everything. There was one night very late, two or three o'clock, when he had sat on one side of the bed and a mournful and lovesick jazz trumpeter had sat on the other, neither willing to leave the other alone there, and all that night he had read aloud into the smell of sandalwood the life story of a mad woman from Butte, Montana. *I, Mary MacLean*, that one was called.

What an occasion she made of it, laid up by flu, hemmed in by rival young men, covered to the chin in an absurd, high-necked, old-fashioned nightgown, taking aspirin with sips of ginger beer, laughing at them alternately or together with that face as vivid on the pillow as a flower laid against the linen. It was innocence. In that crackpot Bohemian pre-crash wonderful time, it was innocence.

How he and the trumpeter broke the deadlock, what had ever happened to the Tom Stead flurry, what had happened to any of Holly's string of admirers — all gone. She sent them away, or they quarreled at her over their bruised egos, or they grew huffy at finding her always in a crowd. Plenty of self-appointed humming-bird catchers, but no captures.

And yet, maybe . . .

Summer and winter, day and night, were telescoped in his memory. How old would he have been? Twenty? Twenty-one? It must have been near the end of Holly's reign in this apartment, before everything went sour and the de-layed wave of the crash reached them and he left school to go to work and Holly herself went away. There was neither beginning nor end nor definite location in time to what he most vividly remembered. What they were doing, whether there had been a party there or whether they had been out on a date, whether she had roommates then or was living alone, none of that came back. But they were alone in a way they had seldom been.

They must have been talking, something must have led up to it, for there she was with the clarity of something floodlighted in his mind, Holly pressing against him and crying with her face against his chest, clinging and crying and saying — he heard only the refrain, not the garble against his chest — "Kim, Kim, get me out of here! I want to get out of this. This is all no good, I've got to, Kim, please!"

Both the tears and the way she clung excited him. But the game had been played so long by other rules that he went on in the old way, laughing, burlesquing gestures of consolation, patting the crow-wing hair, saying, "There

there, little girl." Inanities, idiocies . . . She wore an evening dress cut very low in the back, and he played his
fingers up and down her spine. He slid his hand in against
her skin, slid it further, expecting the competent twist and
shrug and fending and the laugh that would mean the emo-
tional fit was over. But his hand went on around, clear
around, and with a shock like an internal explosion he found
it cupping the frantic softness of her breast.

Even remembering, all his sensations were shocking to
him. He remembered how smoothly the curve of her side
swelled upward, how astonishingly *consecutive* her body
seemed. Also, also, and almost with revulsion, how rigid
and demanding the nipple of her breast. Innocence — he
had never touched a girl there, never imagined, or rather
had imagined wrong. Stupefied by the sudden admission
to her flesh, made uneasy by the way she crowded and
clung, he stood wrapping her awkwardly, and kissed her
and tasted her tears, and thought with alarm and conviction of Tom Stead and the rumored nude, and was anguished with eagerness to escape.

He could remember not a scrap, not a detail, of how he
got away. She offered herself passionately in his memory,
and that was all. The Peewee Golfer putting his little
white ball up the little green alley of his youth came suddenly upon the sidewinder in the sandtrap, the crocodile
in the artificial lake.

Harris closed the door on the ridiculous and humiliating
memory. It had begun to occur to him that he had been an
extraordinary young man, and very little of what had been
extraordinary about himself pleased him. Innocence?
Well, maybe, though there were more contemptuous names
for it. He had been a fraud, a gargler of whisky he would
obediently not drink. A great yapper with the crowd, but

when the cat stopped running, what a frantic sliding to a stop, what digging not to catch what he was after.

Weakly he tried to prop up the slack thing he had been. He told himself that it was a pose with all of them, the life that revolved around Holly was an absurd and perhaps touching and certainly unimportant part of growing up. Or was it? What might he be at this moment, would he have more or less to regret, if he had taken Holly at her passionate word, married her, lived it, as she was determined to live it in her innocence, dangerously?

The last time he saw Holly she was boarding a train for Seattle, on her way to Shanghai and a job they all publicly envied but would probably not have risked taking themselves. Her life, whatever happened to her, would not have been dull. And yet it might have been more thoroughly wasted than at that moment he thought his own had been.

He had played it the other way, not so much from choice as from yielding to pressures, and he had done the best he could with it. How would he look to Holly now, at this very minute? How had he looked then?

Like a bubble of gas from something submerged and decaying in deep water there rose to the surface of his mind one of Blake's Proverbs of Hell that they had admired together that long-gone Christmas morning. It burst, and it said, "Prudence is a rich ugly old maid courted by Incapacity."

It shamed him to remember, though he half repudiated it. From the life of prudence he had got a wife he loved and respected, children he adored, a job he could do with interest and almost with content. He regretted none of them. But he stood here remembering that moment when Holly stopped playing make-believe, and it seemed to him that his failure to take her when she offered herself was one of the saddest failures of his life. The fact that he might make all the same crucial choices the same way if he had them to make again helped not at all; it did him no good to remind himself that no one could turn in any direction without turning his back on something. The past had trapped him, and it held him like pain.

Angrily he looked at his watch. Past five. Starting for the door, he passed the dead woman's table and saw her calm pale face, the skin delicately wrinkled like the skin of a winter-kept apple, but soft-looking, as if it would be not unpleasant to touch. What was her name, what had she died of, what had she looked like when she wore expression? Who mourned her, who had loved her, what things in her life did they regret or had she regretted? Would they think it disagreeable that a total stranger had been alone with her here staring into her dead face? And in that face what was it that the caution of death enclosed and hid?

The barbaric silver necklace seemed somehow to define her. What it said of frivolity, girlishness, love of ornament and of gaiety and of life, made him like her; the way it lay on the sober black crepe breast preached the saddest lesson he had ever learned.

He thought of how she had been transported and tampered with by McBride, and how further touches of disguise would complete her transformation from something real and terrible and lost to something serene, removed, bearable. Alone with her here, before the arrival of others, before she went away, he felt almost an anguish for this woman he had never known, and a strange gratitude that he had been permitted to see her.

Gratitude, or something near it. And yet as he started for the door he threw a sick, apologetic glance around the room as quiet and empty as a chapel, and at the woman who lay so quietly at its center. He meant to tiptoe out, but he heard, almost with panic, the four quick raps his heels made on the bare floor before they found the consoling softness of the stairs.

impasse

By the time they dropped down off the heights, the reluctant sun, which had hung interminably on the Col de Vence and forced Louis to dodge and shield his eyes as he cramped the Citroën around the curves, had finally been dragged below the rim, and the glare of the day was taken off them. Along the grateful gray edge of evening they bounced through the streets of Nice and onto the highway returning back up the coast.

Out on the water it was still full afternoon. Sails passed like gulls; close in, the bay was creased with the water-bug tracks of paddle boats. But where they drove, the day had quieted, and in the confined car the bickering seemed to have quieted, too. Straightening out with the traffic toward Monte Carlo, a drink, dinner, Louis appraised the lengthening silence and grew halfway hopeful.

But he said nothing; the quiet was too pleasant. Only in the sloping windshield he saw the reflection of his wife's face, the mouth drawn down ruefully, and he dropped his hand from the wheel to cover hers. That got him a wan, surprised smile.

Pretending to stretch, he focused his daughter's face in the rearview mirror. No smile there, wan or otherwise. Margaret sat like a captive barbarian queen. Her hair stood up from her forehead in an abrupt black mane. Her eyebrows were heavy, level, finely outlined. Photographs always showed her handsomer than she was, perhaps because photographs, like his shadowed view of her in the mirror, obscured the coarse and roughened skin. But no photograph ever hid what he could not miss now — the arrogant curl of her mouth, the way her eyes looked flatly out in insolence and challenge.

Not a pretty girl. That, of course, was a good part of the trouble. In the windshield he surprised on his own face the rueful, puzzled expression he had seen on his wife's. He heard their friends saying, "How I envy you your three months in France. And how nice you could arrange to take Margaret. How wonderful for all of you, especially for her."

The mildness of evening drifted down off the hills, the first faint, perfumed stirring of the land breeze. Through trees and across gray headlands he saw villas clinging like balconies on the mountain, and turning to see what view they would have, he found Cap Ferrat floodlighted, sharp and cleanly colored, its white villas and red roofs, gray shore and blue encircling sea drenched in light. It seemed to have emerged that minute from the water, wet and fresh. Stuck behind the stinking exhaust of a bus, he watched the promontory, and forgetting that they were silent and at odds, he said, "Somerset Maugham has a villa out there somewhere."

Jean looked, interested. She had read everything Somerset Maugham ever wrote. But from the back seat, Louis heard what he knew he should have anticipated — the contemptuous noise and the voice. "What are we supposed to do about *that*? Make a pilgrimage?"

Patience, he told himself. Aloud he said lightly, "Nothing as strenuous as that, I guess."

"Everybody's got a villa around here someplace, the King of Sweden and the Aga Khan and the Duke of Windsor and King Farouk — everybody you ever heard of. Why go into a tizzy about an old hack like Maugham?"

"Did I go into a tizzy?" Louis said.

"Anyway, how did we get so superior to a great writer all of a sudden?" Jean said, turning half around. "If we're taking that tone, what's so fascinating about King Farouk?"

"I didn't say he was fascinating."

"You implied he was a whole lot more fascinating than Maugham."

"That wouldn't be hard," Margaret said, and turned from the discussion, leaning out the window and raising her indifferent eyes to the hanging houses of Eze Village high on their crag. Louis opened and closed his hands on the wheel and pulled around the bus.

Curving through Villefranche, they looked across the harbor and saw the slim shapes of three destroyers — beautiful, precise toys. The waterfront was dotted with the white figures of sailors.

"Why, they're American," Jean said.

"The Mediterranean Fleet's visiting for a few days. I saw it in the paper." He waited for some contradiction from Margaret, thinking, If she doesn't say something contentious, it'll be the first time since we came here.

But she was silent, and they climbed, circling a hill, and left that harbor and came above another, and there, too, were ships — two more destroyers, a cruiser, and a tanker. The ragged stone of the mountains pitched down to the man-smoothed cirque of the town and its sea fortress, and on a sudden impulse Louis cramped the steering wheel and turned down a steep, narrow street into Beaulieu.

"Where are you going?" Jean said.

"I thought we might have a drink and maybe dinner here. Is there any reason we have to go back to the hotel?"

She glanced at him curiously, but said nothing. He had a feeling that she was thinking exactly what he was — that anything was better than going back to their suite and being alone with their child.

And what a melancholy pass that was, he thought, as he parked and held open the door. Margaret had always been too much for them. It was as if she were dedicated to revenging herself on them for something, as if her rebellious spirit, which turned on everybody in blind, competitive rage, turned most of all on them.

Looking at her now, her dress wrinkled across her too-heavy hips, her face too strong for a girl's, her hair too blue-black, her skin too rough, Louis felt a sad emptiness, a consciousness of failure and loss. Am I to blame? he asked her or himself or the world. Is it my fault you were born unattractive? How much blame shall parents take for begetting and rearing a child? Is that the matter? Do you resent being born? Or have we compounded failure for eighteen years in your bringing-up?

Touched by pity and love, he took an arm of each of his women to escort them across the street; but Margaret pulled her elbow free and walked alone into the open street along the quay, looking into the doors of cafés and cabarets, from which the noise of American jazz erupted. The street was full of sailors, most of them young, hurrying toward something they were very eager about. Their laughter and loudness insulated them, as if behind a layer of glass; they poured by, unseeing; not one so much as looked at the slouching girl who moved along the wall, and she paid no attention to them.

As Jean and Louis turned onto the quay between awninged cafés and shops on one side and the oily harbor water on the other, Jean said, "She'll just make everybody miserable till she gets her way. She's already spoiled the trip for me. I almost wish we could go home."

"Would it be any better there?" he said. He steered her toward the beckoning finger of a waiter in the last café on the quay, and as he seated her, he saw her biting her lip, close to tears. "What would you like to drink?" he said.

"I don't care. Anything."

"Vermouth cassis?"

"All right."

"Two," he told the waiter, and sat down.

For a while, it was as if they were calm. Across the cobbled street a moored barge rocked and thumped softly against the stone. A half-dozen shrill, bare-legged boys played tag from barge to shore and back again. Down by the corner at which they had entered the waterfront, a Navy launch was unloading sailors. A pair of shore patrol sauntered and watched. The waiter brought their drinks and turned over two saucers. Margaret had wandered past all the cheap shops and was now wandering back again.

"Is she ever going to come and sit down with us?" Jean said.

Louis moved his shoulders. "She has to punish us, I expect."

"I wish I knew what for."

"You know what for."

Her eyes, suddenly full again of weak tears, sought his across the table. "How could we fail so badly?" she said. "She's rude, isn't she? She's insolent and rude, and she hates people and lets them know it. Why? You're not that way, and I don't think I am. Where did she learn it?"

Shrugging his shoulders down over his drink, Louis brooded without answering. He remembered how, when Margaret was a child, he had imagined her grown up, imagined them dining out, the attractive girl fresh and interested and warm, clear colored and with candid eyes, and he protective, gravely courteous, the two of them watched by people because of the obvious trust and gentleness between them. He saw himself standing to help his tall daughter into her wrap, moving with her among the crowded tables of such a sidewalk café as this, in some fashionable international place that would delight her. With his elbows on the table, his hands around the cool glass, he looked up and saw his lumpish, arrogant daughter standing above him with her discontent like alum in her mouth.

He rose, pulled out the chair next to him, and said to her gently, "Sit down, Margaret."

"I'd rather stand."

Jean put in, "Please, you must be tired, dear," and got only an overbearing stare.

Quietly Louis sat down again. A bell clinked rapidly, and the launch started with a roar and swung in a speeding arc toward the cruiser.

After a few seconds its wake spread under the barge and set it to knocking hollowly on the stone. The little French boys squealed and leaped aboard. Sometime before the barge stopped pitching, Margaret abruptly sat down. "I'd like a drink."

Wordlessly Louis signaled the waiter, and when he came,

waited wordlessly for his daughter to order. He would not have risked asking her what she wanted.

She kept the waiter standing for thirty seconds and then tossed him the order without looking at him. "Martini, very dry."

The waiter had a dark, smooth face with a prominent widow's peak that looked and might have been the prow of a wig. Stumblingly, not knowing whether or not you said s'il vous plait to waiters, but determined to say it anyway in penance for Margaret, Louis said in his careful school French, "If you please, two more vermouth cassis and the dinner menu." He couldn't tell whether the waiter was grateful or contemptuous or wore impassiveness like his apron, to keep him from being soiled.

The light was withdrawing; the paved curve of quay and fortifications and the town lost their clean outline in smoky dusk. The ships in the harbor had been prematurely lighted for fifteen minutes; now street lights popped on palely, and one after another the shops glowed. A new load of sailors pulled up to the dock, unloaded, stood in line before the money-changing booth under the eyes of the shore patrol. From a half dozen unseen streets music and talk and laughter emptied onto the dock. The new arrivals seized their handfuls of francs and took off. Their white hats were over their eyes, their walks were shore-leave swaggers.

Louis watched them half in amusement, half in distaste. The irrepressible young heading for a binge, they went past in threes and sixes, and talk poured from them. Of an almost comic variety, little ones and big ones, heavy and light, dark and fair, snake hips and fat hips, they moved with one mind and one compulsion. What are they after? he thought. What do they hope to find? The ancient, waiting town took them in as it had taken sailors from the ships of two thousand years. They would not be different from others; their money and their seed would flow in the same abundance, and the town's ancient professions, ancient beds, ancient stones, would accept these, too. The dusk that was rising from buildings and streets and thickening the air along the quay hummed faintly with the revels of antique ghosts.

Jean stirred with a forlorn attempt at comfort and relaxation. She loved coziness; the slightest intrusion of peace into their domestic circle could delude her into gratification. "This is nice," she said. "This was a nice idea, Papa."

He nodded, not to tempt Providence with talk. With Margaret along, conversation was too dangerous. She terrorized them; she was like a rodeo cowboy waiting at the gate, ready to burst out on any bewildered steer of opinion that showed in the arena. If you said anything, affirmed anything, denied anything, liked or disliked anything, you grew horns for her to throw you with.

But she astonished him by saying, "It's at least got it over that phony ritziness at Monte Carlo."

Incautious pleasure was in the look Jean threw Louis. "It has, hasn't it?" she said. "You know, maybe we should move here, if we don't like it there."

"I'm willing."

"All right, let's! It isn't so full of tourists, either."

"Plenty of tourists in sailor suits," Louis said.

"They'll be gone. They don't count. Let's come tomorrow!" Her warm eyes rested on Margaret, slouching in her chair, and something sly moved the corners of her mouth. "Isn't it cool all of a sudden?" she said. "You'll have to grant that the Riviera has *something* nice about it, after all."

"It's all right," Margaret said.

"Maybe it's even as nice as Paris."

Without moving from her slouch, Margaret abandoned docility. Louis could see it happen. "You couldn't resist, could you?" she said. "You had to work in that I-told-you-so. Mother *did* know best, didn't she? Look at the pretty ships, see the handsome sailors. Paris was only a passing fancy, after all, wasn't it?" Like an irritated wild animal — maybe a buffalo, Louis thought, hypnotically watching her — she heaved erect to say loudly, "Paris was *not* a passing fancy! This place is *not* as good as Paris! I can put up with it, but don't feed me that Mother-knows-best stuff!"

"Well, for the love of heaven," Jean said, "what brought on that outburst?"

Margaret gave her a venomous look. "That was no outburst. That was a statement of fact. This place is *not* as good as Paris. I couldn't be less interested in this place. I'm still going to study in Paris next year if it's the last thing I do." Like a truck driver on a narrow road, she crowded Jean into the ditch.

"It's impossible to talk to you," Jean said shakily. "It gives you pleasure to be rude and headstrong. I think you like to hurt us. As for Paris, that's the maddest kind of foolishness."

"Good God, please!" Louis said. The waiter came with the menus, and he ordered dinner for all of them without asking what they wanted. They could eat what they got, *escalopes de veau*, or whatever else. At least they could avoid argument on that.

It was all but dark now; darkness rose from the water to meet the dusk seeping down from the hills; between the two darks the harbor moved in steely glints and darts of red and green. Its sound was a companionable mutter against the quay. On the outer rim of their now dark-enclosed world the ships hung like Christmas decorations, the path that encircled the fort was a half circle of lemon-yellow globes. The mild and misty air took and diffused the light of their water-edged street; from the darker side streets he heard the tom-toms and the squeals. The very thought of all that hopped-up gaiety made him tired. He felt middle-aged and cornered.

With ironic wonder he reflected that some parents, from their children's happy infancy to their successful maturity, had only experiences that inspired affection and pride. Some bright children had no personality problems; they actually liked school, instead of having vomiting spells at six, breaking windows at eight, stealing supplies at ten, defying the teachers at twelve. Some parents had yet to be visited by advisers and child psychologists, who talked of unused capacities and maladjustment and lack of motivation, and who snooped for conflicts in the child's home life and advised more warmth and companionship, the creation of security.

Security! Her parents had created so much security that she could defy them and everything in the world. The very look on her mouth now told him she was coming at him like a fullback.

"How about it?" she demanded.

"How about what?"

"Paris."

"But, Margaret darling, be sensible," Jean said. "What would you do in Paris?"

"Study art," Margaret said, her unblinking eyes on her father.

"Look, Maggie," he said, "has any art teacher in any of

your schools told you you had talent?"

"None of them would have known enough to recognize it."

"But you recognize it in yourself."

"Not recognize it, no. I never really *tried* to paint."

"That's what's so foolish!" Jean cried. "I never heard of anything so — "

"Did I ever try anything I didn't do?" she said, still watching Louis. Her nostrils tightened, her lips thrust out in a thin, fierce line. "Maybe I haven't tried very many things, really. Maybe I never gave a damn. But when I set out to beat that snotty Gerhard kid on the rifle team, I did it, didn't I? The only girl that ever made the rifle team. And when I wanted to be editor of the paper, I got to be, didn't I, over the dead bodies of all the snobs in that journalism class?"

"Those weren't exactly major triumphs," he permitted himself to say, thinking that no accomplishment had ever given her pleasure. The only thing that gave her pleasure was to win out over someone she scorned. And she scorned everybody; she walked on prostrate necks. At any minute the ego that steamed inside her could boil over and scald somebody. "Determination is one thing; talent is another," he said quietly.

"*Opportunity* is what I'm talking about," she said. "Do those stupids with the beards have talent? All those phonies we saw sitting around the Flor or imitating Burl Ives in the Lapin Agile?"

"Do you want to be a stupid with a beard?"

"You know what I mean. If they've got a right there, I sure have. How do I know whether I've got talent unless I try? I'll make talent. I can do anything I make up my mind to."

"Maybe so, maybe so."

"You could try back home," Jean said. "There are art teachers at home. Paris is just not a place for a young girl alone. And you've still got three years more of college."

"Oh, young girl alone!" Margaret said. "College! Good heavens! This is the twentieth century. Grow up and wipe off your chin."

Jean jerked back and pinched her trembling lips together. "Margaret, you're insufferably rude! I can't even talk to you."

"Why try, then?" Margaret said, her hard, intractable eyes fixed on Louis. She had not glanced at her mother since making her demand.

He started to slap his hand on the table, caught himself in time, and laid it down softly. She was where she had always loved best to be, backed into a corner with the dogs at her. Her spirits rose to that sort of thing. With his hand pressing the cool marble, he said, "You are insufferable. Now be still, before you make a scene."

Perhaps because he said it quietly, she sagged back and indifferently shook and côntemplated the olive in her glass. At a certain point she raised the glass and tossed the olive into her mouth. The waiter came with hors d'oeuvres.

The French word that covered so many things nudged itself into Louis' mind as he watched her sulk — *formidable*, maybe even *magnifique*, if you cared for the type. Medea might have been one of these, or Clytemnestra, or Lady Macbeth — all the murderer-queens. But what was he thinking? His child.

Their eyes met, and she said, "I'm sorry, Father."

Instantly he was touched. "Of course," he said. "We all are. But it's your mother you should speak to."

"I'm sorry, Mother," Margaret said.

Jean patted her hand; tears were beaded on her lashes.

So the food that had gone down the throat in ragged, insoluble lumps began to taste better. Louis ordered a bottle of Beaujolais. They remarked on the trick by which the wake of the incoming launch caught all the lights of town and ships and poured them down its rolling trough. They were pleasantly uncrowded; only half a dozen tables in the quayside cafés were occupied. The quay lay open and empty, like a stage.

Into the opening between the *escalopes de veau* and the salad, Louis inserted what he thought of as a simple act of justice and a chance for everybody to close off the bitterness of the recent conversation. Margaret knew she had gone too far; in her more quelled mood she could be talked to reasonably.

"You know we wouldn't deny you anything in reason, if we thought it was good for you, Maggie. But you've never had the slightest interest in art. You have to admit it looks like a whim, because you were excited by Paris."

"It's no whim."

"You've got brains and determination, maybe even talent. But you're only eighteen. Wait till you finish college. Besides, it would cost a lot of money we don't have."

"I could live cheap in Paris."

"Not any more."

"I could work, then."

"At what?"

"I'd find something."

"And if you worked, when would you study art?"

"At night, or after work, or before work. There'd be some time free, for heaven's sake."

He shook his head. "There's a limit to human energy."

"Not to mine."

On the empty stage of the quay a character appeared — a bit player, a walk-on. He came out of the muted revelry of a side street all by himself, a slim young sailor walking the exact middle of the street. His head was down, his white hat was pushed back to expose dark, clustered curls. Concentrating with a seriousness that showed in every move of his body, he came on; his legs buckled him forward, jerked him upright, wobbled him to the left, kinked him back to equilibrium, buckled him forward again. He seemed to have four-way hinges in his knees; his hands hung like things carried in paper bags. As he passed the money-changing booth, the shore patrol moved out alertly. When they took his elbows, he collapsed as if they had kicked his feet from under him. Carefully, more like nurses than police, they dragged him to the wall and propped him on a bench. He leaned and fell off, and they propped him up again.

After two minutes, three more sailors came into the lighted space, the two on the outside supporting the middle one like football players assisting a hurt teammate off the field. They turned him over to the shore patrol, talked for half a minute, and with their hats over their eyes headed at a fast walk back where they had come from. There was still revelry in them; they were still after something. Only the two casualties and a doleful warrant officer with packages beside him and his nose in a comic book inhabited the disciplined area of the dock.

"Thank heavens, you're not a boy and have to go into the service," Jean said. "I should think their officers could control them better. Those boys can't have been ashore two hours."

"It doesn't take long if you work at it," Louis said.

"It's pretty disgraceful all the same," she said. "Do you think we ought to go before they all come back like that?"

"Oh, Mother, relax," Margaret said. "They're making a liberty, for heaven's sake. They've probably been stuck aboard ship for two or three months. This is like in *Mister Roberts*. They're free, for a change."

"Free to make an awful spectacle of themselves. I wonder what the French think."

"Oh, hell!" Margaret said. Her eyes burned oddly, her dark, twisted face thrust forward from the shadows where she sat.

An uncertain silence fell upon them.

At last Jean stood up. "I think I'll hunt up a bathroom," she said abruptly. "Margaret?"

"No," Margaret said. Her eyes were absently fixed across the mistily lighted street. For several minutes she and her father sat in silence.

"I guess we're your prison, aren't we, Maggie?" Louis said at last.

Her hawklike face, handsome in the dusk, snapped around. "What?"

"Paris doesn't really mean art; it means freedom. Isn't that it?"

"Maybe," she said. "It's meant that for a lot of people."

"Stupids with beards?"

"More than those."

"Yes," he said, "I suppose it has." For a while there seemed nothing to say. In spite of her hostility, this was his daughter; he loved her, she anguished him, she broke his heart. He wanted to help her. Finally he said, "Your mother would be heartbroken to think the home she's tried to make for you has been a prison."

Margaret made a deprecatory motion with her hand.

"I could sympathize more with your wish for liberty if I knew what you expected liberty to do for you."

"How do I know till I try?"

"I'm surprised that it's Paris," he said. "Paris is such a stereotype. I shouldn't have thought you'd be taken in by it."

"Stereotype or not," she said.

"Lord, Lord," he said wearily. "Well, we'll see. Your mother will take a good deal of convincing."

So, to his astonishment, he had given in, weakly and behind Jean's back. He looked at his single-minded daughter almost with horror. Yet how could they not give in? How could they hold her? She would slip the collar or chew the leash and be gone in spite of them.

When Jean returned, they were deep in a silence that on his part was sheepish and guilty. She looked at them sharply, perhaps to see if they had been quarreling, and sat down with a sigh. No sooner had she seated herself than two new shore patrol came onto the stone-floored stage, escorting three sailors, one with a smeared blouse and a bloody nose, and all with the signs of belligerence upon them. The patient guardians of the dock accepted these, too, adding them to the casualties on the bench.

"I should think — " Jean started.

Louis, looking to see what had stopped her, saw a tanned, grinning face, a bristly white crew cut, white eyebrows, a rakish hat, a pair of square red hands knuckled on the table top.

"Hi," the sailor said. "I mistaken, or you folks Americans?"

"Are we as obvious as all that?" Jean said, smiling up at him glassily.

"Heard you talkin'," the sailor said. "It sounded good. Where you folks from?"

"Illinois," Jean said. "Aurora."

"That over by Chicago someplace?"

"Very near."

"Well, well," he said. "I'm from Pennsylvania myself — Wilkinsburg — practically part of Pittsburgh."

"My," Jean said with her glassy smile, "we're all a long way from home."

"You ain't kiddin'," the sailor said. "Been here long?"

"Two days. We're staying at Monte Carlo."

"Ha!" He ducked his head, leaning his weight heavily on the table, and looked around at them carefully. "If I'd of had time, I'd of gone. Lots of boys did. They all want to be the guy that busts the bank at Monte Carlo."

"They don't have to go there," Margaret said. "There are casinos in all these towns." She was sitting back in the shadow of the awning, but Louis could see the proud head, the strong profile.

The sailor was giving her his full attention. "Don't I know it," he said. "These French crap games are brutal."

Struck by something in Margaret's voice, even in the way she sat, Louis said impulsively, "Buy you a drink?"

The sailor straightened up easily, loose-shouldered, and Margaret bent forward into the flaky light to turn an empty chair.

The sailor looked at her with his half-shut eyes, grinning amiably. "No, thanks," he said. "I got to go see if I can get me one of these tortoise-shell cigarette cases for my girl friend. They got 'em here for three hundred francs, come from Capri or somewhere." He raised a polite hand to each of them in turn. "Take it easy, now," he said, and passed on with only a slight roll and an excessive dignity to show the load of alcohol he carried.

Jean laughed in relief. "Pleasant enough boy," she said.

"I expect anything from the United States looks good to him."

In pity Louis watched Margaret. She had leaned back again into obscurity, but he knew the sailor's casual rejection burned her like thrown lye. She would be savage and untouchable the rest of the evening.

And what had happened so undramatically was forever beyond talk. He could never say to her, "I saw you invite him, and I saw him take one good look and pass." Could you say to your daughter, "Accept your looks for what they are?" Could you tell her, "You were born struck out, and it won't help to stand in the batter's box demanding that the pitcher throw you a fourth strike?"

In anguish he watched her armor herself with scorn; but what dismayed him was not the scorn but what had for a moment been revealed. Somewhere, back in secret daydreams unknown to anyone, most of all hidden from the parents who were her prison, she had lounged in cafés and joints with longhaired, irresponsible, reckless companions; she had walked with a lover on the Ile St. Louis, and watched the lazy river and lazier fisherman from the Pont Neuf; she had heard the whisper of passion in dark doorways; she had mounted dark stairs with an arm around her and kisses hot upon her lips.

My God, she has *hope*, he said to himself. Everybody young has hope.

It seemed a pathetic and tremendous thing. At that moment he would have given anything if he could have hired someone to make love to his daughter and bring to pass every denouement her mother feared. Yet he knew that the Margaret she would find in Paris would be the same Margaret she had hated and had tried to flee at home.

He could say none of it. He could only, watching from the sad reductions of middle age, let her go, and expect almost with anger that the prison she would flee would sometime become a refuge and a sanctuary.

The launch was coming in, its powerful, water-muffled roar rising against the piled stone of the town. The barge lifted and knocked against the quay. Somehow, while he wasn't watching, the street had filled with sailors, and now they crowded aboard, subdued. The shore patrol herded in the intractables and lifted in the casualties. One gave the launch's bow a hard shove with his foot. The bell clinked, and the motor opened from an idling chuckle to the full-throttle roar as the launch swung out swiftly toward the lighted outlines of the ships pinned against the dark.

"Shall we be getting along?" Louis said.

the
volunteer

WHEN my Latin teacher said she had always wanted a scale model of a Roman *castra* so that pupils reading about the campaigns against the Helvetians could see exactly how the legions built their defenses, of course I volunteered. I was always volunteering. The year must have been 1922. I was thirteen years old, two years behind myself in physical growth, two years ahead of myself in school. Around the high school I drew two kinds of attention, one kind from teachers and another from boys, especially big boys and most especially stupid ones. These last I ignored, or tried to, and I cultivated the praise of the teachers, which was easy to win. Nevertheless, I suppose I would have given considerable to be big and stupid so that I too could sneer at my little peaked face focused on the teacher ready to cry answers, and my little skinny arm flapping at every call to special duty.

A *castra*? I'll make one! I said. I know a slough where there's good clay. I'll get some tonight after school.

Now that, David, said Miss Van der Fleet, is the spirit I like to see.

I lived at the southeast edge of town, where the streets faded out into truck gardens and lucerne fields. The slough was at the southwest, a long two miles added to my walk home. A month before, I had made another volunteering expedition out there to get hydras and paramecia and amoebas for my zoology teacher, but this trip, in late November, was not quite the sunny autumn holiday the other had been. By the time I was laying my books on dry ground at the edge of the slough the afternoon was already late and blue. The wind went dryly through tules and yellow grass, and the sky over the mountains was the color of iron.

It was too cold to take off my shoes and wade. I had to hop from hummock to hummock until I found a place wet enough to dig in. The clay lay under the sod like blue icy grease; it numbed me to the wrists as I filled my lunch pail. I saw a mouse dart through the reeds, and the sad cry of a marsh hawk coasting over made me feel little and alone, and wish that I had brought someone along. I had to remind myself that though it was less fun to do things alone, there was more distinction in it that way. And anyway, who would have come?

The slimy clay stuck like paint on my hands, and it was impossible to get to open water where I could wash. I wiped them as well as I could on the grass, but I had a hard time, working with wrists and elbows and the very tips of my fingers, trying to get my books tucked down inside my belt without smearing them and my clothes with mud.

My way home led across fields and down country roads with few houses. As I came down off the slope the day grew bluer and colder, the wind cut my face, my hand carrying the heavy lunch pail stiffened into an iron hook. Every time I shifted the pail from hand to hand I had to stick out my stomach hard to keep the books from sliding down inside my corduroy knickers. If they had slipped I wouldn't have dared, with those hands, to get them out.

The heroic and indispensable feeling I had started with, the spirit Miss Van der Fleet liked to see, had leaked away. I was not really a hero. I was thin and pale, weak, stick-armed, a cry baby. And no matter how I hawked and snuffled, no matter how many times I tried to clear my nose through my mouth, a clammy and elastic gob began to droop lower and lower on my upper lip.

My muddy frozen claws couldn't have handled a hand-kerchief if I had owned one; they couldn't even have got it out of my pocket. Working my face against the sting and stiffness of the wind, holding my stomach pouted out against books and belt, miserably snuffing and spitting, I went crabwise homeward down a road, across a field, past a yard where a dog leaped out roaring. At last I came to the big cabbage field, still unharvested, that covered many acres just west of us, and passed it with my face sideward to the wind so that the cabbages made changing ranks and then diagonals and then new ranks down the gray field; and finally, my shoulder blades aching and my arms dead and my hands numb and bloodless under the mud, I made it through our sagging picket fence and up onto our ginger-bread-framed porch.

There was a car in our drive: there often was; I was too far gone to pay it any attention. The books were held only by one slipping corner, the clot sagged frantically under my nose. It was like a nightmare in which you have to get to some special safe place before whatever is behind you makes its grab. This time I made it to the door, fell against the jamb and braced the books there. Some rule would be violated, something would happen bad, if I set the pail of mud down until I was clear inside. I hung on to it, braced against the jamb and jamming my frozen thumb at the bell.

Down each side of our door, relic of some time when this had been a fairly pretentious country house, went a panel made up of leaded panes of glass of many colors. Through a violet one just level with my eyes was a neat bullet hole. Nobody knew how it had come there. It hinted of old crimes, feuds, jealous lovers, better days. Sometimes, inside the hall, you could feel through it a thin cold secret draft like the stream of air a dentist squirts into a cavity just before he fills it. Now I put my tongue to the bullet hole, but there was no draft, only cold glass. I remembered that the doorbell hadn't worked since last week, and raised my dirty fist and pounded. Instantly such pain went through my frozen knuckles that I moaned in fury and kicked on the door.

The books slid down inside my pants leg. The clot drooped a dangerous eighth of an inch. Then my father opened the door.

He was very annoyed. "Have you lost the use of your hands?" he said.

Desolately snuffling, tilted into agonies by the contrary strains of the heavy pail in my hand, the heavy books in my pants, I whined, "I was all muddy."

For a second he looked me over in silence; his look was like a hand in the scruff of my neck. Then he said, "What's the matter with your handkerchief?"

He was extraordinarily fussy about things like that. A snuffly nose or somebody who smacked at the table or the sight of someone's dirty fingernails could drive him half wild. And I *had* gone off to school again without a hand-kerchief. I said once more, "I'm all *mud!*"

Somehow I sidled past him into the hall, wonderfully warm with the dry breath from the register. But I didn't dare set down the pail or relax, so long as he was looking at me that way. "Jesus Christ," he said finally. "Thirteen years old and running around with a lamb's leg under your nose making mud pies."

That stung. I whirled around and howled, "I was not! I'm supposed to make a *castra!*"

"Oh, you are," he said. But he was stopped for the moment. I knew he hadn't the slightest idea what a *castra* was, and he wasn't going to ask me and expose his ignorance. I knew things that he hadn't even heard of: that was a sweet fierce pleasure. In the parlor somebody had started to play my new victrola record, a piece called "Nobody Lied," with a big slaptongue baritone sax solo embedded in it. The clot drooped again and I dragged wetly at it, my nose stuffed shut with the sudden warmth of the hall. My father's lips turned inside out. He gave me a push on the shoulder. "Go get yourself cleaned up, and stay out of the front room. There's company."

He didn't need to tell me. Company meant there were people in there buying drinks. That's what we were, a speakeasy. About the time I was born my father was running the same sort of thing in Dakota, but there it had been called a blind pig. I had no desire to go into his crummy parlor, but I said to myself that I wished his damn company would quit wearing out my new record. I started for the kitchen, spraddling because of the books in my pants, and my father said after me, "For God's sake, have you messed your pants too?"

That really made me bawl. I started yelling, "No! My books slipped down, I was just . . . " But he shut me up with one furious motion of his hand. The kitchen door opened and my mother, with an instant cry, stooped to help me: I had finally made it home. Behind me I heard my father saying something humorous to the company.

"Great day," my mother said, "you've got yourself tied hand and foot. What on earth . . . "

She wiped my nose. She pried the pail out of my frozen fingers. She slid my belt buckle open and reached down and got the books. Then she stood me at the sink and ran warm water on my hands until they stung and tingled and grew clean and red while I snarled and complained. Last she rubbed lotion into the bleeding cracks in the backs of my hands and put me at the kitchen table and made me a cup of cocoa.

All I would tell her when she asked what I had been doing and why my lunch pail was full of mud was that my Latin teacher wanted me to make a *castra*. What was a *castra*, she asked, and I flew out at her bitterly. It was a thing for school, a thing the legions built, what did she suppose? Finally she found out that it was something I was going to build with clay on some sort of board base, and she gave me her extra breadboard to build it on. Before supper I spent an intent hour, sitting stocking-footed soaking up the pouring heat from the kitchen register, drawing a *castra* to scale on the clean bleached wood.

Life in our house was full of tensions. For one thing, we were always afraid of the law, and for that reason moved often, even though every move meant losing customers who would never find us again. For another, my mother was the wrong woman to be the wife of a speakeasy owner. She had been brought up in a decent Presbyterian family in Nebraska, and though she wasn't religious she had a full, even a yearning belief in honesty, law, fairness, the respectabilities of family life. When company came she most often stayed in the kitchen; if the party in the parlor grew loud she sat wincing as if she had cramps, and threw looks at me, with little grimaces and jerky movements of hands and shoulders. She was a worn, humble, and decent woman married to the wrong man. Unless my memory is all wrong, I never saw a sadder, more resigned face.

My father was a perfectionist, of a kind; he aspired to run a classy and genteel joint. Even in the ratty old tin-wainscotted, congoleum-floored places we rented he went around with a towel on his arm, always flicking and dusting things, cranking the Victrola, tidying up, making conversation, setting up a free one for good spenders. When, as sometimes happened, he needed help, he expected my mother or me to hop: nothing was more important than the customer's desires. He could fly into a fury over a two-minute delay.

Still, I escaped him all day by going to school, and at home I found it convenient to have loads of homework. At home I was not a volunteer. My mother, having no such escapes, sat next to what she hated and hoped it would not make demands on her or me; for we were, though we never talked openly about it, in mutinous league against our life.

That night new customers came in after five. My father took his plate into the dining room, which could be shut off by sliding doors from the parlor but from which he could hear them if they wanted anything. My mother and I ate in the kitchen. Once, coming in for hot water to make a toddy, he stood in the doorway talking for a moment. He parted his hair in the middle and slicked it down on both sides like an old-fashioned bartender. I honestly think he had a sense of vocation. As he stood flicking his towel I saw his eyes drift over to the table where my breadboard lay with its walls and ditch half molded and its wad of blue clay in the middle. His glance came back across mine like saw teeth across a nail. Through the register, sounding plain but far away, there was the dark, remote throbbing, the last beats of the slaptongue sax, and the voice started chanting, with what seemed inappropriate vivacity,

Nobody lied when they said I cried over you.
Nobody lied when they said that I most died over you.
Got so blue I scarce know what to do . . .

"Don't you want some pie?" my mother said.

"Later," he said, and left.

After supper I went straight back to the *castra.* I wanted to take it to school with me in the morning and dazzle Miss Van der Fleet with the speed of my accomplishment, and force reluctant admiration from the big and stupid, and set the girls a-twitter. One girl in that class thought I had a roguish face; somebody had told me. That word was like a secret twenty-dollar bill in a deep inner pocket that no one knew of. Carefully I went on smoothing the greasy clay into walls, gates, rows of little tents. I would make such a *castra* as Caesar and all his legions had never thrown up in all the plains and mountains of Gaul — roguish I, that brilliant boy, with the spirit the teachers liked to see.

Behind me my mother tipped the coal scuttle into the stove. From the sound I knew there was nothing in it but coal dust and papers, but I did not rise and get her a new bucket of coal. I bent my head and worked on, and I worked in great absorption while she went past me and the door let a cold draft across my neck and closed again, while the returning scuttle knocked against the jamb and then went solidly down on the asbestos stove mat. Later there was a noise of dishes in a pan, a smell of soap and steam: nothing disturbed me. Eventually she stood behind me and I heard the dry rubbing of a towel on china. "Oh," she said, pleased, "it's a kind of little fort!"

"It's a *castra*," I said in scorn. "A Roman camp."

"Have your pie now, I've kept it warm," my mother said about seven o'clock. He took the slab in his clean, round-nailed hand. "Who's in there?" she said.

"Just Lew McReady and his lady friend, now."

"His lady friend. One week he's here with his wife, and the next with his lady friend. Which one, that nurse?"

"Yeah."

"I wonder if she knows he's got children seventeen years old."

"Oh, Lew's all right," he said. "He just likes a change."

He was trying to kid her, but she wouldn't be kidded. She gave him a queer, mixed, unbelieving look. "What a life we lead!" she said. "What friends we have!"

"If you can't tell the difference between a friend and a customer," said my father, "you don't know which side your bread's buttered on."

"Maybe that's the trouble. Maybe all we have is customers."

"If we're starting that again," he said, "I'm going back to the dining room and read the *Post*."

With a push of the shoulder he was gone from the doorway, and my mother looked at me and smiled bleakly. I made no response except to go on smoothing with the back of a paring knife the triangular bits of clay that served as tents. Their wrangling was not a concern of mine. I did not live at that house. I lived at school, where teachers lighted up when I came around and girls thought I had a roguish face. In this country of the enemy inhabited by hostile barbarians I erected my defenses and mounted guard.

"It's beginning to look real good," my mother said after five minutes of clock-ticking, stove-ticking, tap-dripping silence. "You do a nice neat job of things."

Praise made me more businesslike. "I wish I had a little eagle," I said.

"A what?"

"An eagle. Legion standards had eagles on them. In camp they planted the standard in front of the commander's tent."

"I guess . . . I don't quite know what a standard is?" she said. I did not even bother to answer her.

For a while she read a magazine at the other kitchen table. I had not heard any noise, either from my father in the dining room or from the company in the parlor, for some time. The radiator puffed its warm breath against my legs, the dust-puppies fluttered in its grill, the tin pipes sighed and popped. "I've got a pin shaped like a bird," my mother said. "Would that help you? Maybe you could fasten it onto this . . . standard . . . some way."

She bothered me, always trying to horn in on this thing she didn't even understand. On the other hand, maybe I could use the pin. I leaned back. "Let's see it."

"We'll have to wait till they go, in there. It's in my sewing basket."

"I think they're gone."

"I haven't heard the door."

"They're gone," I said. "I'd hear them through the register."

"Well, but . . ." I was already up, skating in stocking feet across the slick linoleum. "Well, all right," she said. "I'll have to find it for you. You'd never know where."

Down the darkish hall, lighted only by a high dim bulb that brought a dull shine out of the newel post and tangled the shadows of the coatrack, I stroked with skating strides, made a detour to pass my hand across the cold stream of air at the bullet hole, and slid up to the open parlor door.

I was there just a split second before the tap of my mother's heels startled them. Lew McReady was bent far over his girl on the sofa, whispering in her ear or kissing her, I couldn't see. But I could see, in the spread of light that the table lamp shed, the white satin softness of the lady friend's blouse, and Lew McReady's hand working like a cat's claws in it.

Then they heard. McReady snapped around and spread his arm in a big elaborate gesture along the sofa back, and yawned as if he had just been roused from a nap. The girl made a sound like a laugh. Behind me my mother said in a tight, strained voice (had she seen?), "I'm sorry, David needed something for a thing he's making for school. Excuse me . . . just a second . . . he's making something . . ."

McReady crossed his legs and made a sour mouth. I knew his son at high school, one of the big stupid ones, a football player who was supposed to star if he ever got eligible. But I couldn't stay looking at McReady; I had to stare at the nurse, who smiled back at me. She seemed extraordinarily pretty. I could not understand how she could be so pretty and let old McReady paw her. She had a laughing sort of face: and she was lost and damned.

She said, "What is it you're making?"

"A *castra* — a Roman camp."

"For Latin?"

"Yes."

My mother was rummaging through the sewing basket; I wished she would bring the whole thing so we could escape from there, and yet I was glad for every extra second she took. McReady lighted a cigarette, still spread-eagled elegantly over the couch. He had a red face with large pores and the hair on top of his head was very thin, about twelve hairs carefully spread to cover as much skull as possible. When he took the cigarette from his lips and looked at the tip and saw lipstick there he put the back of his hand to his mouth and looked across it and saw me watching him. So he separated himself from us and interested himself in a long wheezing coughing spell; his eyes glared out of his purpling face with a kind of dull patience, waiting for things to die down. The nurse smiled at me, and, loathing her, I smiled back. She said, "I took Latin once. 'Gallia est omnis divisa in partes tres.' "

"My Go-guho-guhod!" McReady said through his coughing, his bulging eyes staring at her glassily. "An unexpec-uhec-uhected talent!"

My mother was surprised too. I saw both her surprise and her pleasure that something from the world of my school meant something to somebody, even though she herself couldn't share it and even though the one who could was this lady friend of McReady's. Maybe she was as mixed about this girl as I was, and I was truly mixed. I could still see that hand in her breast, and the softness under the satin was like the voluptuous softnesses that coiled around me in bed some nights until I lay panting and glaring into the dark, feeling my ninety-pound body as hot and explosive as if my flesh had been nitroglycerin packed on my bones. This girl looked at me with clear eyes, she had several wholesome freckles, she laughed with a dimple. Above all she quoted Caesar (and what if it was only the first line, it was correct: most dopes said *omnia* instead of *omnis*). I could hardly have been more shaken if I had run into Miss Van der Fleet having a snort of Sunnybrook Farm in our parlor. Actually that would have shaken me less, for Miss Van der Fleet would never crawl naked and voluptuous through my dreams, and this one would, oh, this one would!

I said sullenly and stupidly, "Quarum unum incolunt Belgae."

"Lucy," Lew McReady said, "we are dealing with a pair of real scholars." His face, mocking me, was exactly the face of any number of the big and stupid at school. I hated him. I hated his whiskey breath and his red mocking face and the memory of his hand in this lost girl's breast. I hated the way he called my mother by her first name, as if she was some friend of his. I hated everything about him and he knew it.

"Ma," I said passionately, "I got to . . ."

"Yes," she said, coming along but hesitating, out of politeness, for a few more words. "You'd think the world depended on it," she said to the nurse. "He's fixing this *castra* and he needed a bird for the standard. That's what we came in to get. School is awful important to him," she said with an abrupt, unexpected laugh. "If I didn't chase him out to play he'd study all the time . . ."

The dining room door slid back and my father came in. His eyes were heavy on my mother and then me, but just for an instant. He said heartily, "Well, well, old home week. Everything O.K.?"

"Just getting ready to beat it," McReady said.

My father flicked his towel across his hand. "One for the road?"

"Naw, we got to go," McReady said. He wadded out his cigarette, looking down with smoke still puffing from his mouth and nose and drifting up into his eyes, and the elk's tooth on his watch chain jiggled with his almost noiseless wheezing.

The nurse rose. "I bet he's bright in school," she said. (And what did her smiling mean as she looked from my mother to me? Did she find my face roguish?)

My mother said, "We hadn't been here a month till they moved him ahead another grade. He's only thirteen. He won't be quite sixteen when he graduates."

I could have killed her, talking about me in front of everybody with that proud proprietary air. Their eyes were all on me like sash weights: my mother's full of pride, the nurse's smiling, with a question of some kind in them, my father's speculative, McReady's just dull and steady and streaked. Then McReady picked up a book from the end table by the sofa and knocked it on his knuckles. "This something you read for school?" he said.

The book was mine, all right. They must have been looking at it earlier, and seen my name in it. It was by Edgar Rice Burroughs, and it was called *At the Earth's Core*. It was about a man who invented an underground digger in which he broke through the crust of the earth and into the hollow inside, where there was another world all upside down and concave instead of convex, and full of tyrannosauri and pterodactyls and long-tailed people covered with fine black fur. So McReady cracked it open and of course it opened to the page I had most consulted, a picture of the tailed furry girl who fell in love with the hero. She didn't have anything on.

He showed it around, and he and my father laughed and the nurse smiled and shook her head and my mother smiled too, but not as if she felt like it. "You better stick to Latin, kiddo," McReady said, and dropped the book back on the table.

All my insides were pulled into a knot under my wishbone. I think I must have shivered like a dog. If asked, I suppose I could have given a very logical explanation of why McReady chose to humiliate a runty thirteen-year-old: I was too much smarter than his own dumb son, I had walked in on his necking party, I might talk. On the last he might have saved his worry. About things that happened in my non-school life I never said anything, not a word. But though I could have explained McReady's act, I didn't survive it. It paralyzed me, it reduced me to a speck in front of them all, especially that girl. I left them laughing — some of them were laughing, anyway — and vanished. By the time they left I was back at the *castra* in the kitchen.

Almost at once I heard my parents. Their voices came plainly through the kitchen register.

"What went on in here?" my father said. "Something drove him away. He was good for all night."

"He was good for all night if we provided a bed for him and his lady friend," said my mother's strange, squeaky trembling voice. It burst out in a furious loud whisper. "What a thing for him to see in his own parlor! Oh, Buck, I could . . . if we don't . . ."

"What are you talking about? Talk sense. What went on here? What do you mean?"

"I mean," she said, "Lew and that girl. We came in to get something from my sewing basket, and they were so — they didn't even hear us coming. His hands were all over her. David couldn't help seeing, because *I* saw, and I was behind him."

The register sighed with the empty rush of air. Then he said, "Well God Almighty, I've told you a hundred times to keep him out of there. How the hell do you suppose people like to have kids peeking around the corners at them when they're out partying? Kids who know your own kids, for God's sake! Do you think you'd ever come back? Not on your life. Kiss him goodbye . . . and he was good for ten or fifteen dollars a week every week. Oh, God *damn*, if either of you had the sense of a . . ."

My hands were shaking so that I could hardly stick the match stem down into the clay before the commander's tent. When I pressed the pin down into the end of the wood I split it clumsily, and snatched it and threw it furiously away. My mother was saying out of the register's warm rush, "Will you tell me why — just tell me why — a boy should have to stay out of part of his own home, and hang out in the kitchen like the hired girl, for fear of what he'll see if he doesn't? Is that the way a home should be? How can he grow up right, or have any self-respect, or even know what's right and wrong, when all he sees at home is people like Lew McReady?"

The sigh and steady rush of air. My father said, "This is a place of business, too, remember? This is how we make a living. We stop this we don't eat."

"Sometimes I think I'd rather not eat," she said. "So help me God, I'd rather starve!" In the tin insides of the register something boomed like a drum. My mother said, "I wonder how we'll feel if he turns out bad? What if we make him into a thief, or something worse? Do you want him to be like . . ."

"Like me?" he said, in a voice so soft and ugly that I held my breath.

"I'm as guilty as you are," she said, and the register

boomed so that with all my straining I heard only a mumble for a second, and then words again, ". . . fifteen years to pretend it was only bad times, something temporary, you'd get into something decent. But Buck . . . I'm . . . there's a limit."

"Yes," he said heavily, "I guess there is."

I sat with my eyes squeezed half shut and my ears trying to repudiate the quarreling voices, frozen in some frantic, desolated rejection of everything that surrounded and threatened me. The humiliation of a few minutes before was still sour as bile in my throat, and now this new outburst of an old quarrel, the threat of separation and breakup. What would happen to me, did they ever think of that? I would be pulled out of school, everything I lived for would be yanked away from me. It wasn't fair. Quite suddenly the *castra* with its *vallum* and its ditch and its rows of tents swam distorted and watery. I ground my teeth in shame and rage. It wasn't fair. The register was silent. I could imagine them in there, speechless.

Blindly I kicked my feet into my shoes under the table, bent on getting out, but a noise at the hall door made me whirl around. My mother came quietly in. In the one wild glance I threw I saw only her still, white face. She smiled, and her voice was low, almost matter of fact. "Does it work all right?" she said.

It took me a moment to understand that she was talking about the pin. "No," I said then. "It's too big. It splits the match." Accusingly I glared at her where she wavered in the big lens of tears.

"Why Davey!" she said. "You're crying! Oh, poor little kid!"

She started for me, but I yanked my sweater from the hook and tore open the outside door. Down the steps I lurched and recovered and ran and stopped in the shadow where the old pear tree tangled its branches with the overgrown lilac hedge. My mother's silhouette was back there in the lighted rectangle of the door. "Davey!" her high voice said. After that one cry she stood very still, not calling, seeming to listen. Then with her head bowed she turned back in, and the rectangle of light and the glimpse of lighted kitchen like a Dutch painting narrowed and was gone.

Under the pear tree's darkness it was still and cold; when I went out through the hole in the hedge I saw my breath white against the light from the corner. I stood there with my fists clenched and my teeth clenched and my mind clenched against the sobs that rattled and shook me, and it was some time before I stopped crying. Then as I raised my head I heard the faint distant rush and hum of traffic from uptown, but immediately around me there was not a sound. It was as if we lived not merely at the edge of town but outside the boundaries of all human warmth, all love and companionship and neighborliness, all light and noise and activity, all law.

I had never been able to bring a friend home from school. Once, when a good-natured bigger boy rode me home on his handlebars, I gave him the wrong address and stood at a strange gate until he disappeared. The very sight of that dark house, divided within itself, but enclosing its total secret behind thick hedges, closed doors, drawn blinds, shook me with desolation and self-pity. I set off up the sidewalk, which after half a block became a dirt path, and as I walked I cursed aloud in a methodical filthy stream.

I cursed my father and Lew McReady and the wicked girl who had started all this; she was as repulsive to me as if I had seen her copulating with animals. I shed tears for my mother and for myself, forced to live in a way we hated. After a while, exhausted with tears and cursing, under trees that rattled stiffly in a little night wind, I stood imagining revenges, triumphs, ways of growing rich. I magnified myself in years, strength, wealth, confidence, nerve. I whipped my father with my tongue and mind till he cried and begged my pardon for all he had ever done against me and all the impatience and contempt he had ever had for my weakness. At one point I made him stand at one side while I broke all his bottles of homemade Sunnybrook until the cellar swam with whiskey and he was kneedeep in broken glass. I switched away from that to destroy Lew McReady, going on along the dark path stumbling and erratic, my mind full of carnage. I saw McReady in a dozen postures of defeat, collapse, unconsciousness, cowardly begging. I saw the girl, too; she came up to me soft and beguiling, and my image of her was totally obscured for a moment by the picture of my own scornful eyes and the twist on my mouth as I repudiated her. Would I touch anything that McReady had touched? But within seconds after that magnificent rejection I was thinking how it would be to touch her, and I was beside her in some very private place with a grate fire when I came to myself and fell to cursing again. When I thought of how close I had come to admitting that nurse, or letting her lure me, into those dreams of voluptuousness and concupiscence, I shook with self-loathing. Passing a tree, I smashed my fist against it and howled with instant fury at the pain.

There was a moon like a chip of ice; the air smelled of smoke and frost. I was the loneliest creature alive. With my hands tucked under my sweater armpits, my eyes glaring bleakly into the dark, shaken occasionally with a long shuddering diminishing sob, I went on. Now I was at the edge of the big cabbage field I had passed that afternoon. Out of pitchblack shadow the heads lifted their even rows, touched by the moon with greenish light.

Reminded of the *castra* with its even rows of tents, I yearned for that job I had begun. I wanted to be back there safe above the warm register, removed, intent, and inviolate. I saw the warm lighted kitchen then as a sanctuary; though I had fled from it, I had had enough already of loneliness and cold and dark. And anyway what I had really fled from was in the parlor. In the kitchen-sanctuary was not only the light and warmth but the true thing that made it sanctuary: my mother, sitting with her magazine, glancing across from her isolation to mine, making tentative, humble suggestions that might for a moment gain her admittance to the other world I escaped to.

It seems to me that understanding and shame dawned on me together, coming on gradually like the rheostat-controlled light in a darkened theater. I had had all the contempt I wanted, that day, and yet I began then to heap more on myself, and not only to accept it but almost to relish it. With my chin on a fencepost I stared out across the glimmering cabbage field and gnawed my chapped knuckles, thinking, admitting, condemning myself. There was this one person in the entire world who loved me wholly, only this one that I could wholly trust. And if I thought myself lonely, desolate, friendless, abused, what should I think of her? I had my escape, and I was almost as used to praise as to contempt. Outside my hateful house I had been able to gather praise with both hands, and bring it back to her and have it doubled. But who praised her? Who helped her? What did she have?

My father said, *How else would we eat? Did you ever hear of money?*

It would be better to starve, my mother said. *So help me God, I'd rather.*

I won't let us starve, I said. *I'll get a job. I'll quit school if I have to. I'll . . .*

Roguish I, the ninety-pound volunteer.

In the thin moonlight the cabbages went row on row like the crosses in the poem; their ranks swam and melted and re-formed greenishly, shadowily, a great store of food left carelessly unplucked, while in our house we ran a speakeasy because it was the only thing my father knew how to do, and my mother submitted because she must — perhaps because of me. In my nostrils, shrunken by the cold, lay the sourish smell of the field. I dove under the fence and in a moment was wrestling with an enormous cabbage, trying to unscrew its deep root from the ground. Before I defeated it I was crying again with anger and exhaustion, but there it lay at last, a great cold vegetable rose. Stripping off the outer leaves, I rolled it under the fence, crept through after it, gathered it in my arms, and went staggering toward home.

I heard the phonograph the moment I opened the door; my mother was sitting alone in the kitchen. Her life was right where I had left it. As I stuck my head and half my body into the light and warmth she jerked to her feet, and her eyes went from my face to the front of my sweater where dirt from the cabbage root had rubbed off on me, and from that to my hand, still out of sight holding the cabbage behind the door jamb.

"Where did you go?" she said. "Are you all right?"

Already my confidence in what I had done was leaking away; the last block of the way home, the cabbage had weighed like solid lead. It seemed to me that all that day

I had been carrying weights too heavy for my arms up to that house I hated and took refuge in. Now by its root I dragged the upended head around the door, and searching her face for her response, I said, "I brought you something."

She was standing straight by her chair. Her head did not move as she glanced at the cabbage; only her eyes flicked down and then back. She said nothing — not "Oh, how nice!" or even "Where did you get it?" Nothing.

Panic began to rise in me, for here in the kitchen I couldn't pretend that the cabbage was anything but ridiculous, a contribution to our household that would have made my father snort in incredulous contempt. Moreover — and this was worse because it concerned her, not him — it had been stolen. She knew at once it was a theft I offered her. I remembered her angry whisper coming with the rush of air through the register: *I wonder how we'll feel if he turns out bad? What if we make him into a thief, or worse? How will he ever be able to tell right from wrong?*

"Ma . . ." I said.

It was more than I could do to support her still look. Still clutching the cabbage, I let my eyes wander away until they settled upon the *castra*. There lay reassurance: the daubed walls were tight and neat, the tents lay in mathematically precise rows. Like a dog on a track my mind ducked to one side, and I found myself repeating other words like *castra* that had a different meaning in singular and plural — words like *gratia-gratiae*, and *auxilium-auxilia*, and *impedimentum-impedimenta*, and *copia-copiae* — and even going over some of the words that customarily took *in* with the accusative: names of towns, small islands, *domus, rus*.

Out of the register came the squawk of a record ending,

a big burst of laughter, a woman's squeal, shouts whose words I resolutely would not hear, then the music again: good old "Nobody Lied," my own contribution to the parlor fun. I brought my eyes around again to her, opening my mouth to say, "I . . ." She was still looking at me intently; her hands hung awkwardly before her as if she had forgotten them there. Her mouth twitched — smile, or grimace such as she made when the parlor got rowdy?

Perhaps the true climax of that rueful day and that rueful period of our lives is this tableau in which I after a fashion present and she in some sort accepts the grotesque vegetable I have stolen to compensate her for the wrongs and uncertainties and deprivations of her life. I bring her this gift, this proof of myself, and we stare at each other with emotions mixed and uneasy. What shall we say there in that kitchen? What another family might greet with great belly laughs we cannot meet so easily. We have no margin for laughter.

The slaptongue sax is pounding and throbbing through the pipes. I want to say to her, I am awful, I have filthy thoughts, I steal, I would even cheat if I couldn't get A any other way. I'm a cry baby and people laugh at me and I'm sorry I . . .

I say none of it. She says, with her eyes glittering full, "Ah, poor Davey," and puts up her arms and I creep into them, and I suspect that, hugging each other in the sanctuary kitchen, we are both about half comforted.

field guide
to the
western birds

I MUST SAY that I never felt better. I don't feel sixty-six, I
have no gerontological worries; if I am on the shelf, as
we literally are in this place on the prow of a California hill,
retirement is not the hangdog misery that I half expected
it to be. When I stepped out of the office, we sold our
place in Yorktown Heights because even Yorktown Heights
might be too close to Madison Avenue for comfort. The
New Haven would still run trains; a man might still see
the old companions: I didn't want to have to avoid the
Algonquin at noon or the Ritz bar after five. If there is anything limper than an ex-literary agent it is an ex-literary
agent hanging around where his old business still goes on.
We told people that we were leaving because I wanted to
get clear away and get perspective for my memoirs. Ha!
That was to scare some of them, a little. *What I Have
Done for Ten Percent.* I know some literary figures who
wish I had stayed in New York where they could watch me.

But here I sit on this terrace in a golden afternoon, finish-
ing off an early, indolent highball, my shanks in saddle-

stitched slacks and my feet in brown suede; a Pebble Beach pasha, a Los Gatos geikwar. What I have done for ten percent was never like this.

Down the terrace a gray bird alights — some kind of towhee, I think, but I can't find him in the bird book. Whatever he is, he is a champion for pugnacity. Maybe he is living up to some dim notion of how to be a proper husband and father, maybe he just hates himself, for about ten times a day I see him alight on the terrace and challenge his reflection in the plate glass. He springs at himself like a fighting cock, beats his wings, pecks, falls back, springs again, slides and thumps against the glass, falls down, flies up, falls down, until he wears himself out and squats on the bricks panting and glaring at his hated image. For about ten days now he has been struggling with himself like Jacob with his angel, Hercules with his Hydra, Christian with his conscience, old retired Joe Allston with his memoirs.

I drop a hand and grope up the drained highball glass, tip the ice cubes into my palm, and scoot them down the terrace. "Beat it, you fool." The towhee, or whatever he is, springs into the air and flies away. End of problem.

Down the hill that plunges steeply from the terrace, somewhere down among the toyon and oak, a tom quail is hammering his ca-whack-a, ca-whack-a, ca-whack-a. From the horse pasture of our neighbor Shields, on the other side of the house, a meadowlark whistles sharp and pure. The meadowlarks are new to me. They do not grow in Yorktown Heights, and the quail there, I am told, say Bob White instead of ca-whack-a.

This terrace is a good place just to lie and listen. Lots of bird business, every minute of the day. All around the house I can hear the clatter of house finches that have nested in the vines, the drainspouts, the rafters of the carport. The liveoaks level with my eyes flick with little colored movements: I see a redheaded woodpecker working spirally around a trunk, a nuthatch walking upside down along a limb, a pair of warblers hanging like limes among the leaves.

It is a thing to be confessed that in spite of living in Yorktown Heights among the birdwatchers for twenty-four years I never got into my gaiters and slung on my binoculars and put a peanut butter sandwich and an apple in my pocket and set off lightheartedly through the woods. I have seen them come straggling by on a Sunday afternoon, looking like a cross between the end of a YWCA picnic and Hare and Hounds at Rugby, but it was always a little too tweedy and muscular to stir me, and until we came here I couldn't have told a Wilson Thrush from a turkey. The memoirs are what made a birdwatcher out of Joseph Allston; I have labored at identification as much as reminiscence through the mornings when Ruth has thought I've been gleaning the busy years.

When we built this house I very craftily built a separate study down the hill a hundred feet or so, the theory being that I did not want to be disturbed by telephone calls. Actually I did not want to be disturbed by Ruth, who sometimes begins to feel that she is the Whip of Conscience, and who worries that if I do not keep busy I will start to deteriorate. I had a little of that feeling myself: I was going to get all the benefits of privacy and quiet, and I even put a blank wall on the study on the view side. But I made the whole north wall of glass, for light, and that was where I got caught. The wall of glass looks into a deep green shade coiling with the python limbs of a liveoak, and the oak is always full of birds.

Worse than that for my concentration, there are two casement windows on the south that open onto a pasture and a stripe of sky. Even with my back to them, I can see them reflected dimly in the plate glass in front of me, and the pasture and the sky are also full of birds. I wrote a little thumbnail description of this effect, thinking it might go into the memoirs somewhere. It is something I learned how to do while managing the affairs of writers: "Faintly, hypnotically, like an hallucination, the reflected sky superimposed on the umbrageous cave of the tree is traced by the linear geometry of hawks, the vortical returnings of buzzards. On the three fenceposts that show between sky and pasture, bluejays plunge to a halt to challenge the world, and across the stripe of sky lines of Brewer's blackbirds are pinned to the loops of telephone wire like a ragged black wash." I have seen (and sold) a lot worse.

I am beginning to understand the temptation to be literary and indulge the senses. It is a full-time job just watching and listening here. I watch the light change across the ridges to the west, and the ridges are the fresh gold of wild oats just turned, the oaks are round and green with oval shadows, the hollows have a tinge of blue. The last crest of the Coast Range is furry with sunstruck spikes of pine and redwood. Off to the east I can hear the roar, hardly more than a hum from here, as San Francisco pours its commuter trains down the valley, jams El Camino from Potrero to San Jose with the honk and stink of cars, rushes its daytime prisoners in murderous columns down the Bayshore. Not for me, not any more. Hardly any of that afternoon row penetrates up here. This is for the retired, for the no-longer-commuting, for contemplative ex-literary agents, for the birds.

Ruth comes out of the french doors of the bedroom and

hands me the pernicious silver necklace that my client Murthi once sent her in gratitude from Hyderabad. The bird who made it was the same kind of jeweler that Murthi is a writer: why in *hell* should anyone hand-make a little set screw for a fastener, and then thread the screw backwards?

I comment aloud on the idiocy of the Hyderabad silversmith while I strain up on one elbow and try to fasten the thing around her neck, but Ruth does not pay attention. I believe she thinks complaints are a self-indulgence. Sometimes she irritates me close to uxoricide. I do not see how people can stay healthy unless they express their feelings. If I had that idiot Murthi here now I would tell him exactly what I think of his smug Oxonian paragraphs and his superior sniffing about American materialism. If I hadn't sold his foolish book for him he would never have sent this token of gratitude, and all the comfortable assumptions of my sixty-six years would be intact. I drop the screw on the bricks: *invariably* I try to screw it the wrong way. Cultural opposites; never the twain shall meet. Political understanding more impossible than Murthi thinks it is, because the Indians insist on making and doing and thinking everything backwards.

"No fog," Ruth says, stooping. At Bryn Mawr they taught her that a lady modulates her speaking voice, and as a result she never says anything except conspiratorially. A writer who wrote with so little regard for his audience wouldn't sell a line. On occasion she has started talking to me while her head was deep inside some cupboard or closet so that nothing came out but this inaudible thrilling murmur, and I have been so exasperated that I have deliberately walked out of the room. Five minutes later I have come back and found her still talking, still with her head among the coats and suits and dresses. "*What?*" I am inclined to say then. The intent is to make her feel chagrined and ridiculous to have been murmuring away to herself. It never does. A Bryn Mawr lady is as unruffled as her voice.

"What?" I say now, though this time I have heard her well enough. It just seems to me that out on the terrace, in the open air, she might speak above a whisper.

"No fog," she says in exactly the same tone. "Sue was afraid the fog would come in and chase everybody indoors."

I get the necklace screwed together at last and sink back exhausted. I am too used up even to protest when she rubs her hand around on my bald spot — a thing that usually drives me wild.

"Are you ready?" she says.

"That depends. Is this thing black tie or hula shirt?"

"Oh, informal."

"Slacks and jacket all right?"

"Sure."

"Then I'm ready."

For a minute she stands vaguely stirring her finger around in my fringe. It is very quiet; the peace seeps in upon the terrace from every side. "I suppose it isn't moral," I say.

"What isn't?"

"This."

"The house? What?"

"All of it."

I rear up on my elbow, not because I am sore about anything but because I really have an extraordinary sense of well-being, and when I feel anything that strongly I like a reaction, not a polite murmur. But then I see that she is staring at me and that her face, fixed for the party, is gently and softly astonished. It is as definite a reaction as they taught her, poor dear. I reach out and tweak her nose.

"I ought to invest in a hair shirt," I say. "What have I

done to deserve so well-preserved and imperturbable a helpmeet?"

"Maybe it's something you did for ten percent," she whispers, and that tickles me. I was the poor one when we were married. Her father's money kept us going for the first five or six years.

She laughs and rubs her cheek against mine, and her cheek is soft and smells of powder. For the merest instant it feels *old* — too soft, limp and used and without tension and resilience, and I think what it means to be all through. But Ruth is looking across at the violet valleys and the sunstruck ridges, and she says in her whispery voice, "Isn't it beautiful? Isn't it really perfectly beautiful!"

So it is; that ought to be enough. If it weren't I would not be an incipient birdwatcher; I would be defensively killing myself writing those memoirs, trying to stay alive just by stirring around. But I don't need to stay alive by stirring around. I am a bee at the heart of a sleepy flower; the things I used to do for a living and the people I did them among are as remote as things and people I knew in prep school.

"I am oppressed with birdsong," I say. "I am confounded by peace. I don't want to move. Do we have to go over to Bill Casement's and drink highballs and listen to Sue's refugee genius punish the piano?"

"Of course. You were an agent. You know everybody in New York. You own or control Town Hall. You're supposed to help start this boy on his career."

I grunt, and she goes inside. The sun, very low, begins to reach in under the oak and blind me with bright flashes. Down at the foot of our hill two tall eucalyptuses rise high above the oak and toyon, and the limber oval leaves of their tips, not too far below me, flick and glitter like tinsel fish.

From the undergrowth the quail cackles again. A swallow cuts across the terrace and swerves after an insect and is gone.

It is when I am trying to see where the swallow darted to that I notice the little hawk hovering above the tips of the eucalyptus trees. It holds itself in one spot like a helicopter pulling somebody out of the surf. The sparrow hawk or kestrel, according to the bird book, is the only small hawk, maybe the only one of any kind, that can do that.

From its hover, the kestrel stoops like a falling stone straight into the tip of the eucalyptus and then shoots up again from among the glitter of the leaves. It disappears into the sun, but just when I think it has gone it appears in another dive. Another miss: I can tell from its angry *kreeeeee!* as it swerves up. All the other birds are quiet; for a second the evening is like something under a belljar. I watch the kestrel stop and hover, and down it comes a third time, and up it goes screeching. As I stand up to see what it can be striking at, it apparently sees me; it is gone with a swift bowed wingbeat into the sun.

And now what? Out of the eucalyptus, seconds after the kestrel has gone, comes a little buzzing thing about the size of a bumblebee. A hummingbird, too far to see what kind. It sits in the air above the tree just as the kestrel did; it looks as if it couldn't hold all the indignation it feels: I think of a thimble-sized Colonel Blimp with a red face and asthmatic wheezings and exclamations. Then it too is gone as if shot out of a slingshot.

I am tickled by its tiny wrath and by the sense it has shown in staying down among the leaves where the hawk couldn't hit it. But I have hardly watched the little buzzing dot disappear before I am rubbing my eyes like a man seeing ghosts, for out of this same eucalyptus top, in a kind of Keystone Kop routine where fifty people pour out of one old Model T, lumbers up a great owl. He looks as clumsy as a buffalo after the speed and delicacy of the hawk and the hummingbird, and like a lumpish halfwit hurrying home before the neighborhood gang can catch and torment him, he flaps off heavily into the woods.

This is too much for Joseph Allston, oppressed with birdsong. I am cackling to myself like a maniac when Ruth comes out onto the terrace with her coat on. "Ruthie," I tell her, "you just missed seeing Oliver Owl black-balled from the Treetop Country Club."

"What?"

"Just as Big Round Red Mr. Sun was setting over the California hills."

"Have you gone balmy, poor lamb?" Ruth whispers, "or have you been nibbling highballs?"

"Madame, I am passionately at peace."

"Well, contain your faunish humor tonight," Ruth says. "Sue really wants to do something for this boy. Don't you go spoiling anything with your capers."

Ruth believes that I go out of my way to stir up the animals. Once our terrier Grumpy — now dead, but more dog for his pounds than ever lived — started through the fence in Yorktown Heights with a stick in his mouth. He didn't allow for the stick and the pickets, and he was coming fast — he never came any other way. The stick caught solidly on both sides and pretty near took his head off. That, Ruth told me in her confidential whisper, was the way I had approached every situation in my whole life. In her inaudible way, she is capable of a good deal of hyperbole. I have no desire to foul up Sue's artistic philanthropies. I can't do her boy any good, but I'll sip a drink and listen, and that's more help than he will get from any of the twelve people who will be there when he finally plays in Town Hall.

II

In California, as elsewhere, alcohol dulls the auricular nerves and leads people to raise their voices. The noise of cocktail parties is the same whether you are honoring the Sitwells in a suite at the Savoy Plaza, or whether you are showing off a refugee pianist on a Los Gatos patio. It sounds very familiar as we park among the Cadillacs and Jaguars and one incredible sleek red Ferrari and the routine Plymouth suburbans and Hillman Minxes of the neighbors. The sound is the same, only the setting is different. But that difference is considerable.

Dazed visitors from the lower, envious fringes of exurbia — and those include the Allstons, or did at first — are likely to come into the Casement cabaña and walk through it as if they have had a solid thump on the head. This cabaña has a complete barbecue kitchen with electrically operated grills thirty feet long. It has a bar nearly that size, a big television screen and a hi-fi layout, a lounge that is sage and gray and tangerine or lobster, I am not decorator enough to tell. It is chaste and hypnotically comfortable and faintly oppressive with money, like an ad for one of the places where you will find Newsweek or see men of distinction.

The whole glass side of the cabaña slides back and the cabaña becomes continuous with a patio that spreads to the edge of the pool, which is the color of one of the glass jars that used to sit in the windows of drugstores in Marshalltown, Iowa, when I was a boy. Across the pool, strung for a long distance along the retaining wall that holds the artificial flat top onto this hill, are the playing fields of Eton. I think I have never toured them all, but I have seen a croquet ground; a putting green; a tennis court and a half-sized paddle-tennis court; a ping-pong table; a shuffleboard court of smooth concrete; and out beyond, a football field, full-sized and fully grassed, that was built especially for young Jim Casement and his friends and so far as I have observed is never used. Beyond the retaining wall the hill falls away steeply, so that you look out across it and across the ventilators of the stables below the wall, and into the dusk where lights are beginning to bloom in beds and borders down the enormous garden of the Santa Clara Valley.

A neighborhood couple of modest means — and there are some — contemplate gratefully their admission to these splendors. A standing invitation amounts to a guest card at an exclusive club, and the Casements are generous with invitations. At some stage of their first tour through the layout any neighbor couple is sure to be found standing with their heads together, their eyes gauging and weighing and estimating, and you can hear the IBM machinery working in their heads. Hundred thousand? More than that, a lot more. Hundred and fifty? God knows what's in the house itself, in which the Casements do not entertain but only live. Couldn't touch the whole thing for under two hundred thousand, probably. A pool that size wouldn't have come at less than ten thousand; the cabaña alone would have cost more than our whole house . . .

I have been around this neighborhood for more than six months, and in six months the Casements can make you feel like a lifelong friend. And I have not been exactly unfamiliar in my lifetime with conspicuous consumption and the swindle sheet. But I still feel like whistling every time I push open the gate in the fence that is a design by Mondrian in egg crates and plastic screen, and look in upon the pool and the cabaña and the patio. The taste has been purchased, but it is taste. The Casement Club just misses being extravagantly beautiful; all it needs is something broken or incomplete, the way a Persian rug weaver will leave a flaw in his pattern to show that Allah alone is perfect and there is no God but God. This is all muted colors, plain lines, calculated simplicities. As I hold open the gate for Ruth, with the noise of the party already loud in the air, I feel as if I were going aboard a brand new and competitively designed cruise ship, or entering the latest Las Vegas motel.

We have not more than poked our heads in, and seen that the crowd is pretty thick already, before Sue spots us and starts over. She has a high-colored face and a smile that asks to be smiled back at, a very warm good-natured face. You think, the minute you lay eyes on her, What a nice woman. And across clusters of guests I see Bill Casement, just as good-natured, waving an arm, and with the same motion savagely beckoning a white-coated Japanese to intercept us with a tray. It is one of Bill's beliefs that guests at a Casement party spring into the splendid patio with bent elbows and glasses in their hands. He does not like awkward preliminaries; he perpetuates a fiction that nobody is ahead of anybody else.

"Ah," Sue says, "it's wonderful of you to come!" The funny thing is, you can't look at that wide and delighted smile and think otherwise. You are doing her an enormous favor just to be; to be at her party is to put her forever in your debt.

I scuff my ankles. "It is nothing," I say. "Where are

the people who wanted to meet me?"

Sue giggles, perfectly delighted. "Lined up all around the pool. Including the next-most-important guest. You haven't met Arnold, have you?"

"I don't think he has met me," I say with dignity.

She has us by the elbows, starting us in. I twist and catch up two glasses off the tray that has appeared beside me, and I exchange a face of fellowship with the Japanese. Then the stage set swallows us. Mr. and Mrs. Allston, Ruth and Joe, the Allstons, neighbors, we are repeated every minute or two to polite inattentive people, and we get people thrown at us in turn. Names mean less than nothing, they break like bubbles on the surface of the party's sound. We are two more walk-ons with glasses in our hands; our voices go up and are lost in the clatter that reminds my bird-conscious ears of a hundred blackbirds in a tree.

Groups open and let us in and hold us a minute and pass us on. My recording apparatus makes note of Mr. Thing, a white-haired and astonishingly benevolent-looking music critic from San Francisco; and of Mr. and Mrs. How-d'ye-do, whose family has supported music in the city since Adah Menken was singing "Sweet Betsy from Pike" to packed houses at the Mechanics' Hall. We shake the damp glass-chilled hand of Mr. Monsieur, whom we have seen on platforms as the accompanist of a celebrated Negro soprano, and Ruth has her hand kissed by a gentleman whom I distinguish as Mr. Budapest, a gentleman who makes harps, or harpsichords, and who wears a brown velvet jacket and sandals.

Glimpses of Distinguished Guests, filets of conversation au vin, verschiedene Kalter Aufschnitt of the neighborhood:

Sam Shields, he of the robust cement mixer and the acres of homemade walks and patios and barbecue pits and incinerators, close neighbor to the Joseph Allstons; home-builder who erected by hand his own house, daring heaven and isostasy, on the lip of the San Andreas fault. With a Navy captain and a Pan-Am pilot, both of the neighbor-hood (the pilot owns the Ferrari) he passes slowly, skinny-smiling, blue-bearded, with warts, ugly as Lincoln, saying: *I do not kid you. A zebra. I rise up from fixing that flat tire and I am face to face with a zebra. I am lucky it wasn't a leopard. Hearst stocked that whole damn duchy with African animals, including giraffes. It wouldn't surprise me if pygmies hunt warthogs through those hills with blowguns* . . . And as he passes, the raised glass, the *salud:* Ah there, Joe!

Four Unknowns, two male and two females, obviously not related by marriage because too animated, but all deco-rous, one lady with cashmere sweater draped shawl-like over her shoulders, the other winking of diamonds as she lifts her glass; the gentlemen deferential, gray, brushed, double-breasted, bent heads listening: *Bumper to bumper, all the way across, and some idiot out of gas on the bridge* . . .

Mrs. Williamson, beagle-breeder extraordinary, Knight of the AKC, leather-faced, hoarse-voiced (*Howdy, Neigh-bor!*) last seen on a Sunday morning across the canyon from the Allstons' house, striding corduroy-skirted under the oaks, blowing her thin whistle, crying in the barroom voice to a pack of wag-tailed long-coupled hounds, *Pfweeeet! Here Esther! come Esther!* Here we go a-beag-ling. Wrists like a horsewoman, maybe from holding thirty couple of questing hounds on leash. Now, from quite a distance, rounding the words on the mouth, with a white smile, brown face, tweed shoulders, healthy-horsy-country woman, confidential across forty feet of lawn: *How are the memoirs?*

More Unknowns, not of the local race. City or Upper Peninsula, maybe Berkeley, two ladies and a gentleman, dazzled a little by the Casement Club, watchful. Relax and pass, friends. It is no movie set, it was made for hospitality. The animals who come to drink at this jungle ford are not what they seem. No leopards they, nor even zebras. Yon beagle-breeding Amazon is a wheelhorse of the League of Women Voters, those two by the dressing-room doors at the end of the pool spend much of their time and all of their surplus income promoting Civil Liberties and World Government. Half the people here do not work for a living, for one reason or other, but they cannot be called idlers. They all do something, sometimes even good. And you do not need, as on Martha's Vineyard, to distinguish between East Chop and West Chop. Here we live in a mulligan world, though it is made of prime sirloin . . . *Ah, how do you do? Yes, isn't it? Lovely . . .*

Bill Casement, with his golfer's hide, one eye on the gate for new arrivals — shake of the head, *Quite a struggle, boy,* stoops abstractedly to listen to a short woman with a floury face. Somebody comes in. *Excuse me, please.* Short woman looks around for another anchorage — turn away, quick.

And what of the arts? Ah there, again, in a group: Mr. Thing, Mr. Budapest, Mr. and Mrs. How-d'ye-do, surnamed Ackerman, a tight enclave of the cognoscenti, on their fringes an eager young woman, not pretty, perhaps a piano teacher somewhere; this her big moment, probably, thrilled to be asked here, voice shaking and a little too loud as she wedges something into the conversation, *But Honegger isn't really — do you think? He seems to me . . .* And to me, thou poor child. You have not gone to heaven, you do not have to prove angelhood, you are still in the presence of mortals. Listen and you shall hear.

And what of the Great Man? He is coming closer. There is a kind of progress here, though constantly interrupted, like walking the dog around Beekman Place and up to 51st and back down First Avenue. Magnetic fields, iron filings, kaleidoscopic bits of colored glass that snap into pattern and break again.

On around the diving board, onto the lawn, softer and quieter and with a nap like a marvelous thick rug. Something underfoot — whoop! what the hell? Croquet wicket. Half a good drink gone — on Ruth's dress? No. To the rescue another Japanese, out of the lawn like a mushroom. Thank you, thank you. Big tooth-gleaming grin, impossible to tell what they think. Contempt? Boozing Americans? But what then of all the good nature, the hospitality, the generosity? What of that, my toothy alert impeccable friend? Would you prefer us to be French aristocrats out of Henry James? Absurd. Probably has no such thoughts at all, good waiter, well trained.

"Ah," Sue says, "there he is!"

It is in her face like a sentence or a theorem: Here is this terrific musician, the best young pianist in the world. And here is this ex-literary agent, knows everybody in New York, owns Town Hall, lunches with S. Hurok twice a week. And here I have brought them together, carbide and water, and what will happen? Something will — there will be an explosion, litmus paper will change color, gases will boil and fume, fire will appear, a gleaming little nugget of gold or radium will form in the crucible.

Mr. Kaminski, Mr. and Mrs. Allston. Arnold, Joe and Ruth.

Now hold your breath.

III

My first impression, in the flick of an eye, is *What in hell can Sue be thinking of?* My second, all but simultaneous with the first, is *Bill Casement had better look out.*

Taking inventory during the minute or two of introductions and Ruth's far inland murmur and Sue's explanations of who we all are, I can't pick out any obvious reason why Kaminski should instantly bring my hackles up. His appearance is plus-minus. His skin is bad, not pitted by smallpox or chickenpox but roughened and lumpy, the way a face may be left by a bad childhood staphylococcus infection. His head is big for his body, which is both short and slight, and his crew-cut hair, with that skin, makes him look like a second in a curtain-raiser at some third-rate boxing arena: his name somehow ought to be Moishe, pronounced Mushy. But he has an elegant air too, and he has dressed for the occasion in a white dinner jacket. His eyes are large and brown and slightly bulging; some women would probably call them "fine." They compensate for his mouth, a little purse-slit like the mouth of a Florida rock fish.

The proper caption for the picture in its entirety is "Glandular Genius." I suppose if you are sentimental about artistic sensibility, or fascinated by the neurotic personality, you might look at a face like Kaminski's with attention, respect, perhaps sympathy and a shared anguish.

He has all the stigmata of the type, and it is a type some people respond to. But if you are old Joe Allston, who has had to deal in his time with a good many petulant G.G.'s, you look upon this face with suspicion if not distaste.

It makes, of course, no difference to me what he is. Nevertheless, Bill Casement had better look out. This pianist is pretty expressionless, but such expression as he permits himself is so far a little shadowy sneer, a kind of controlled disdain. Bill might note not only that expression, but the air of almost contemptuous ownership with which Kaminski wears Sue's hand on his white sleeve. And it does not seem to me that even Sue can look as delighted and proud as she looks now out of simple good nature. It is true that she is as grateful for a friendly telephone call as if it had cost you fifty dollars to make it, and true that if you notice her and speak to her and joke with her a little she is constitutionally unable to look upon you as less than wonderful. It is a kind of idiotic and appealing humility in her: she is as happy for a smile as Sweet Alice, Ben Bolt. But right now she looks at Kaminski in a way that can only be called radiant; no woman of fifty should look at any young man that way, even if he can play the piano. If she knew how she looks, she would disguise her expression. The whole tableau embarrasses me, because I like Sue and automatically dislike the cool smirk on Kaminski's face, and I am sorry for Sue's sake that no chemical wonder is going to take place at our meeting. As for Kaminski, he is not stupid. Within three seconds he is giving me back my dislike as fast as I send it.

Sue stands outside the closed circuit of our hostility like a careless person gossiping over an electric fence.

"People who have so much to give as you two ought to know each other. Though what the rest of us do to deserve

you both is more than I know. It's so *good* of you to be
here! And shall I tell you something, Joe? Do you mind
being used? Isn't that an awful question! But you see,
Arnold, Joe was a literary agent for years and years in New
York — the best, weren't you, Joe? For who? Hemingway?
John Marquand? Oh, James Hilton and James M. Cain
and all sorts of people. And we know he couldn't be what
he was without having a lot of influence in the other arts
too. So we're going to use you, unscrupulously. Or *I* am.
Because it's so difficult to make a career as a concert
pianist. It's as if there were a conspiracy . . . "

She is holding a glass, but does not seem to have drunk
from it. Her hand is on Kaminski's arm, and her face
shines with such goodness that I am ready to grind my
teeth.

It is Ruth's belief that I take instant and senseless dis-
likes to people and that when I do I go out of my way to
pick quarrels. Nothing, in fact, could be more unjust. Right
now I am aching to harpoon this Kaminski and take the
smirk off his face, or at least make him say something dis-
honestly modest, but what do I say? I say, "I'm afraid
you're wrong about my having any influence where it would
count. But we're looking forward to hearing you play." I
could not have bespoke him more fair. He drops his arrogant head a little to acknowledge that I live.

"It's a wonder you haven't heard him clear over on your
hill," Sue says. "All he does all day and night is sit down
in the cottage and practice and practice and practice —
terribly difficult things. He doesn't even remember meals
half the time; I have to send them down on a tray." She
gives his arm a slap — you naughty boy. "And he's got
such power," she cries. "Look at his hands!"

She turns over his hand, which is the hand of a man half

again as big as he is, a big thick meaty paw like a butcher's. The little contemptuous shadow of his expression turns toward her. "If I make too much noiss?" he says. These are the first actual words we have heard him say.

I am not a Glandular Genius. I am not even an Artist, and hence I am not Sensitive. But I can recognize a challenge when I hear one, especially when there is an edge of insult in it. Poor Sue takes his remark, apparently, as some sort of apology.

"Too much noise nothing! If the neighbors hear you, that's their good luck. And when you break down and play Chopin — which is never often enough — then they're double lucky. You know what we did the other night, Ruth — Joe? We heard Arnold playing Chopin down below, to relax after all the terribly difficult things, and we all just pulled up chairs on the patio and had a marvelous concert for over an hour. Even Jimmy, and if you can make *him* listen! Really, *nobody* plays Chopin the way Arnold does."

Arnold's expression says that he concurs in this opinion, though generally opinions from this source are uninformed.

He stands there aloofly, not contaminating his art by brushing too close to Conspicuous Consumption. I am reminded irritably of my ex-client Murthi, who would have been astonished by nothing in this whole evening: he would have recognized it as the American Way from old Bob Montgomery movies. He would have recognized Kaminski too: the Artist (imported, of course — the technological jungle could only borrow, not create) captive to the purse and whim of the Nizam-rich, the self-indulgent plutocracy. Murthi would have welcomed in Kaminski a fellow devotee of the Spirit.

Nothing gives me a quicker pain than that sort of arrogance, whether it is Asian, European, or homegrown. I suppose I am guilty of impatience. Our neighbor Mrs. Shields, who does a good deal of promoting of International Understanding among foreign and native students at Stanford, ropes us in now and then for receptions and such. Generally we stand around making polite international noises at one another, but sometimes we really get a good conversation going. It seems to me that invariably, when I get into the middle of a bunch of thoroughly sensible Indians and Siamese and West Germans and Italians and Japanese and Guamanians, and we begin to get very interested in what the other one thinks, there is sure to come up someone in the crowd with a seed in his teeth about American materialism. This sets my spirituality on edge, and we're off.

It will not do for me to be too close to Kaminski tonight. He has hardly said a word, but I can see the Spirit sticking out all over him.

The Japanese passes with a tray. "Arnold?" Sue says. He makes a gesture of rejection with his meaty hand. He is above a drink. But I am pleased to see that when Ruth engages him in one of her conspiratorial conversations he is as vulnerable as other mortals. He listens with his head bent and a pucker between his eyes, not hearing one damned word, but forced to listen.

Well out of it, I stand back and watch, and remember nights when my ten percent involvement in artists didn't permit me to stand back — such a night as the Book-of-the-Month party when the Time-Life boy got high and insulted his publisher's wife, and punches flew, and in the melee someone — I swear it was a *Herald Tribune* reviewer — bit a chunk out of the lady's arm. She got blood poisoning and nearly died. A critic's bite is as deadly as a camel's, apparently. None of that for me, ever again. Let Art pursue its unquiet way, be content to be a birdwatcher of Los Gatos.

I hear Sue say lightly, "You're so dressed up, Arnold. You're the dressiest person at your party."

And wouldn't that be true, too: wouldn't Caliban, in this crowd where nothing is conventional except the thinking, just have to be correct as a haberdasher's clerk? Oh, a beauty. I bury my nose in a third highball, feeling ready and alert and full of conversational sass, but not wanting to get involved with Kaminski, and having no one else handy. Sue and her pianist are listening intently to Ruth's whisper. Teetering on my toes, I catch fragments of talk from people passing by, and think of Sam Shields and his zebra, and of Murthi again, and of how zebras roaming the California hills would not surprise Murthi at all. He would have seen them in some movie. Spiritually empty Americans are always importing zebras or leopards or crocodiles for pets. Part of the acquisitive and sensational itch. Roman decadence.

The whole subject irritates me. How in hell do zebras get into an intelligent conversation?

Some god, somewhere, says Let there be light, and a radiance like moonlight dawns over the patio and the clusters of guests. A blue underwater beam awakes in the pool; the water smokes like a hot spring. Sue's eyes are on the velvet-coated man, who is describing something with gestures to the music-patronizing Ackermans. One of the neighbors, in a loud plaid tweed, stands aside watching the musicians as he would watch little animals digging a hole. I have a feeling that I have failed Sue; Kaminski and I have already practically dropped one another's acquaintance. Her eyes wander around to me. She looks slightly puzzled, a little tired. She rounds her eyes to indicate how pleasantly difficult all this is, and bursts into laughter.

"Everybody here?" I ask.

"Almost, I think. At least the ice seems to be getting broken. Honestly, I don't know half the people here myself. Isn't that a giveaway? This is the first stock I ever bought in musical society."

"Very pretty party," I say. It is. From across the pool it is strikingly staged: lights and shade, compositions of heads and shoulders, moving faces, glints of glass and bright cloth. For a moment it has the swirl and flash of a Degas ballet, and I say so to Sue. I hear Bill Casement's big laugh; white coats dart around; the Mondrian gate opens to spill four late arrivals into the patio.

"Excuse me," Sue says. "I must go greet somebody. But I particularly wanted Arnold to meet the Ackermans, so I'm going to steal him now. Arnold, will you come . . . "

He stands with his fish mouth flattened; he breathes through his nose; he does not trouble to keep his voice down. He says, "For God's sake, how long is this going to go on?"

Sue's eyes jump to his; her lips waver in an imbecilic smile. Her glance swerves secretly to me, then to Ruth, and back to Kaminski. "Well, you know how people are," she says. "They don't warm up without a . . . "

"Good God!" says Kaminski, in a sudden, improbable rage, gobbling as if his throat were full of phlegm. "I am supposed to play for pigs who swill drinks and drinks and drinks until they are falling-down drunk and then will stuff themselves and sleep in their chairs? These are not people to listen to music. I can't play for such people. They are the wrong people. It is the wrong kind of party, nothing but drinks."

Ruth is already trying to pull me away, and I am pretending to go with her while at the same time holding back for dear life; I wouldn't for a fat fee miss hearing what this monster will say next. Sue swings him lightly around, steers him away from us, and I hear her: "Oh, please, Arnold! There's no harm done. We talked about it, remember? We thought, break the ice a little first. Never mind. I'm sorry if it's wrong. We can serve any time now, they'll be ready to listen as soon as . . . "

I am dragged out of earshot, and wind up beside Ruth, over against the dressing rooms under a cascade of clematis. Ruth looks like someone who has just put salt in her coffee by mistake. With her white hair and black eyebrows, she has a lot of lady-comedian expressions, but she doesn't seem to know which one to use this time. Our backs against the dressing-room wall, we sneak a cautious look back where we have just casually drifted from. Sue's Roman-striped cotton and Kaminski's white coat are still posed there at the far edge of the illumination. Then he jerks his arm free and walks off.

Ruth and I look at each other and make a glum mouth. There goes the attempt of a good-natured indiscreet well-meaning culture-craving woman to mother an artistic lush. Horrible social bust, tiptoes, hush-hush among her friends. Painful but inevitable. She looks forlorn at the edge of the artificial moonlight of her patio. A performance is going on, but not the one she planned. The audience is there, but it will have no recital to attend, and will not see the real show, which is already over.

Now don't be stupid and go after him, I say to Sue in my

mind, but I have hardly had the thought before she does just that. What an utter fool.

That is the moment when the white coats line up in front of the cabaña, and one steps out ahead of the others. He raises his hands with the dramatics of an assistant tympani player whose moment comes only once, and knocks a golden note from a dinner gong.

An arm falls across my shoulders, another sweeps Ruth in. "Come on," says Bill Casement's gun-club golf-course dressing-room voice. "Haven't had a word with you all night. By God, it's a pleasure to see a familiar face. How's it going? O.K.? Good, let's get us some food."

IV

Assembly line along a reach of stainless steel; the noisy, dutiful, expectant shuffling of feet, the lift of faces sniffing, turning to comment or laugh, craning to look ahead. *Mnnnnnnnnn!* Trenchers as big as cafeteria trays, each hand-turned from a different exotic wood. Behind the counter white coats, alert eyes, ready tongs, spoons, spatulas. A state fair exhibit of salads — red lettuce crinkly-edged, endive, romaine, tomatoes like flowers, hearts of artichokes *marinée*, little green scallions, *caveat emptor*. Aspic rings all in a row. A marvelous molded crab with pimento eyes afloat in a tidepool of mayonnaise. Some of that . . . that . . . that.

Refugees from Manhattan. Load these folks up, they haven't had a square meal since 1929.

A landslide, an avalanche: slabs of breast from barbecued turkeys, gobs of oyster dressing, candied yams dripping like honeycomb. A man with a knife as long as a sword and as limber as a razorblade whips off paper-thin slices from a ham, leafs them onto trenchers. Another releases by some sleight of hand one after another of a slowly revolving line of spits from a Rube Goldberg grill. Shishkebab. Tray already dangerous, but still pickles, olives, celery frizzled in crushed ice, a smörgasbord of smoked salmon, smoked eel, smoked herring, cheeses. Ovens in the opulent barbecue yield corn fingers, garlic bread.

No more, not another inch of room — but as we turn away we eye three dessert carts burdened with ice cream confections shaped like apples, pears, pineapples, all fuming in dry ice. Also pastries, petits fours, napoleons, éclairs. Also batteries of coffee flasks streaming bright bubbles. Also two great bowls in which cherries and fat black berries and chunks of pineapple founder in wine-colored juice. Among the smokes of broiling, freshness of scallions, stink of camembert, roquefort, liederkranz, opulence of garlic butter, vinegar-bite of dressings, sniff that bouquet of cointreau and kirsch in which the fruits are soaked. Lucullus, Trimalchio, adsum.

But hardly Trimalchio. Instead, this Bill Casement, tall and brown, a maker and a spender loaded with money from lumber mills in the redwood country; no sybarite, but only a man with an urgent will to be hospitable and an indulgent attitude toward his wife's whims. He herds us to a table, looks around. "Where the hell's Sue?" A man behind the counter flashes him some signal. "Excuse me, back in a second. Any of these musical characters tries to sit down here, say it's saved, uh?" Down-mouthed, with his head ducked, he tiptoes away laughing to show that this party is none of his doing, he only works here.

The lawn where Sue and Kaminski have been standing until just a few minutes ago stretches empty and faultless in the dusk. No hostess, no guest of honor. "Quite an evening," I say.

Ruth smiles in a way she has. "Still oppressed with bird-song?"

"Why don't you save that tongue to slice ham with?" I reply crossly. "I'm oppressed all right. Aren't you?"

"If she weren't so nice it would be almost funny."

"But she *is* so nice."

"Yes," she says. "Poor Sue."

As I circle my nose above the heaped and delectable trencher, the thought of Kaminski's bald scorn of food and drink boils over in my insides. Is he opposed to nourishment? "A pituitary monster," I say, "straight out of Dostoevsky."

"Your distaste was a little obvious."

"I can't help it. He curdled my adrenal glands."

"You make everything so endocrine," she says. "He wasn't that bad. In fact, he had a point. It *is* a little alcoholic for a musicale."

"It's the only kind of party they know how to give."

"But it still isn't quite the best way to show off a pianist."

"All right," I say. "Suppose you're right. Is it his proper place to act as if he'd been captured and dragged here? He's the beneficiary, after all."

"I expect he has to humiliate her," Ruth says.

Sometimes she can surprise me. I remark that without an M.D. she is not entitled to practice psychiatry. So maybe he does have to humiliate her. That is exactly one of the seven thousand two hundred and fourteen things in him that irritate the hell out of me.

"But it'll be ghastly," says Ruth in her whisper, "if she can't manage to get him to play."

I address myself to the trencher. "This is getting cold.

Do we have to wait for Bill?" When I fill my mouth with turkey and garlic bread, my dyspeptic stomach purrs and lies down. But Ruth's remark of a minute before continues to go around in me like an augur, and I burst out again: "Humiliate her, uh? How to achieve power. How to recover from a depressing sense of obligation. How to stand out in every gathering though a son of a bitch. Did it ever strike you how much attention a difficult cross-grained bastard gets, just by being difficult?"

"It strikes me all the time," Ruth murmurs. "Hasn't it ever struck you before?"

"You suppose she's infatuated with him?"

"No."

"Then why would she put up with being humiliated?"

Her face with its black brows and white hair is as clever as a raccoon's. But as I watch it for an answer I see it flatten out into the pleasant look of social intercourse, and here is Bill, his hand whacking me lightly on the back. "Haven't been waiting for me, have you? Fall to, fall to! We're supposed to be cleared away by nine-thirty. I got my orders."

Our talk is of barbecuing. Do we know there are eighteen different electric motors in that grill? Cook anything on it. The boys got it down to a science now. Some mixups at first, though. Right after we got it, tried a suckling pig, really a shambles. Everybody standing around watching Jerry and me get this thing on the spit, and somebody bound to say how much he looks like a little pink scrubbed baby. Does, too. Round he goes, round and round over the coals with an apple in his mouth and his dimples showing, and as his skin begins to shrink and get crisp, damn if his eyes don't open. By God! First a little slit, then wide open.

Every time he comes round he gives us a sad look with these baby blue eyes, and the grease fries out of him and sizzles in the fire like tears. If you'd squeezed him he'd've said mama. He really clears the premises, believe me. Two or three women are really *sick* . . .

Big Bill Casement, happy with food and bourbon, looks upon us in friendship and laughs his big laugh. "Pigs and all, barbecuing is more in my line than this music business. About the most musical I ever get is listening to Cotton-seed Clark on the radio, and Sue rides me off the ranch every time she catches me." He rears back and looks around, his forehead wrinkles clear into his bristly widow's peak. "Where d'you suppose she went to, anyway?"

Ruth gives him one of her patent murmurs. It might as well be the Lord's Prayer for all he hears of it, but it comforts him anyway. Sue and Kaminski are nowhere to be seen — having a long confab somewhere. Thinking of what is probably being said at that meeting, I blurt out, "What about the performer? Who is he? Where'd Sue find him?"

"Well," Bill says, "he's a Pole. Polish Jew," he adds apologetically, as if the word were forbidden. "Grew up in Egypt, went back to Poland before the war, just in time to get grabbed by the Polish army and then by the Nazis. His mother went into an incinerator, I guess. He never knew for sure. I get all this from Sue."

His animation is gone. I am damned if he doesn't peek sideways and bat his eyes in a sheepish way around the patio pretending to be very disinterested and casual. He seems set to start back to attention at any slightest word with "What? Who? Me?"

"Very bright guy," he says with about the heartiness of a postscript sending love to the family. "Speaks half a dozen languages — German, Polish, French, Italian, Arabic, God knows what. Sue found him down here in this artist's colony, What's-its-name. He was having a hell of a time. The rest of the artists were about ready to lynch him — they didn't get along with him at all for some reason. Sue's been on the board of this place, that's how she was down there. She can see he's this terrific prospect, and not much luck so far except a little concert here and there, schools and so on. So she offers him the use of the cottage, and he's been here three weeks."

I watch his hand rubbing on the creased brown skin of cheek and jaw. The hand is manicured. I can imagine him kidding the manicurist in his favorite barbershop. He is a man the barbers all know and snap out their cloths for. He brings a big grin to the shoeshine boy. The manicurist, working on his big clean paw, has wistful furtive dreams.

"You met him yet?" Bill asks.

"We talked for a little while."

"Very talented," Bill says. "I guess. Make a piano talk. You'd know better than I would — artists are more in your line. I'm just a big damn lumberjack out of the tall timber."

In that, at least, he speaks with authority and conviction. Right now he would be a lot more at home up to his neck in a leaky barrel in some duck marsh than where he is.

Now I see Sue coming down along the fence from the projecting wing of the main house. She is alone. She stops at a table, and in the artificial moonlight I can see her rosy hostess's smile. "Here comes your lady now," I say.

Bill looks. "About time. I was beginning to . . . Say, I wonder if that means I should be . . . Where's Kaminski? Seen *him*?"

"Over across the pool," Ruth whispers, and sure enough there he is, walking pensively among the croquet wickets with his hands behind his white back. The Artist gathering his powers. I cock my ear to the sounds of the party, but all is decorous. All's well, then.

"Maybe I better push the chow line along, I guess," Bill says. He raises an arm and a white coat springs from beside the cabaña wall. In a minute we are confronted by a pastry cart full of all those éclairs and petits fours and napoleons and creampuffs. An arm reaches down and whisks my plate away, slides another in. Right behind the pastry cart comes another with a bowl of kirsch-and-cointreau-flooded fruit and a tray of fruity ice cream molds. Forty thousand calories stare me in the face: my esophagus produces a small protesting conscientious *pwwk!* From the pastry man with his poised tongs and poised smile Ruth cringes away as if he were Satan with a fountain pen.

"Pick something," I tell her. "Golden apples of the sun, silver apples of the moon. You have a duty."

"Ha, yeah, don't let that bother you," Bill says, like a man who gets a nudge without letting it distract him from what he is looking at. Sue has stopped at a nearby table to talk to the Ackermans and the white-haired critic and the harpsichord man. The little music teacher, type-cast for the homely sister of a Jane Austen novel, has managed to squeeze into the musical company. It is all out of some bird book, how the species cling together, and the juncoes and the linnets and the seed-eaters hop around in one place, and the robins raid the toyon berries en masse, and the jaybirds yak away together in the almond trees. The party has split into its elements, neighbors and unknown visitors and the little cluster of musicians. And now Sue, bending across them, beckons Kaminski, and he comes around the diving board, the hatchings of some cuckoo egg whose natural and unchangeable use it is to thrust his bottomless gullet up from the nest and gobble everything a foolish foster mother brings.

The rather dour accompanist moves to make place for him. Sue will not sit down: she stands there animated, all smiles. And Kaminski has changed his front. His politeness is as noticeable as perfume. He talks. He shows his teeth in smiles. The little music teacher leans forward, intent to hear.

With a tremendous flourish the waiter serves Ruth a bowl of fruit. "You do that like Alfredo serving noodles," I say, but Ruth, who knows what I mean, does not say anything, and the waiter, who may or may not, smiles politely, and Bill, who hasn't the slightest idea, comes back beaming into the conversation as if glad of any innocent conversational remark. With a bite of éclair in my mouth I wag my head at him, how delicious. I force down a few spoonfuls of ambrosial fruit. I succeed in forestalling ice-cream. The carts go away. Jerry comes around with a coffee flask. I dig out a couple of cigars.

I am facing the musical table, but I have lost my interest in how they all act. Full of highballs, food, smoke, coffee, my insides coil around heavily like an overfed boa constrictor. The only reason I don't slide down in my chair and get really comfortable is that Kaminski is sitting where he can see me, and I will not give him the satisfaction of seeing me contented and well nourished. For his performance I shall make it a point to be as wide-awake as a lie-detector, and though I shall listen with an open mind, I shall not be his most forgiving critic.

But there is a clash between comfort and will, and a little balloony pressure in my midsection. Damn Kaminski. Damn his Asiatic spirituality and his coddled Art and his ghetto defensiveness and his refugee arrogance. My esophagus comes again with a richly flavored *brwwp!* Just an echo, hoo hoo.

"Say," says Bill, "how would a brandy go? Or calvados? I got some damn good calvados. You never had any till you taste this."

The impetuous arm goes up, but Sue, who must have had her eye sharp on him, is there before the waiter. "Bill, do me a favor?"

"Surest thing you know. What?"

"Have Jerry close the bar. Don't serve any more now till afterward."

"I was just going to get Joe a snifter of calvadoes to go with his cigar."

"Please," she said. "Joe won't mind postponing it."

I have not been asked, but I do not mind.

"O.K.," Bill says. "You know what you're doing, I guess. Did you get anything to eat? I kept looking around for you."

"I'll get something later. As soon as people seem to be through, Jerry can start arranging the chairs. I went over it with him this afternoon."

"Check," says Bill. A smile, puzzled, protective, and fond, follows her back to the musician's table. "Bothers her," Bill says. "She's got her heart set on something great. Old Arnold had better be good."

We are silent, stuffed. I commune with my cigar, looking sleepily around this movie set where the standard of everything is excess. Somewhere down deep in my surfeited interior I conduct a little private argument with my client and conscience, Murthi. He is bitter. He thinks it is immoral to fill your stomach. In India, he tells me, the only well-fed people are money-changers and landlords, grinders of the faces of the poor. But these people, I try to tell him, grind no poor. They are not money-changers or landlords. They are the rich, or semi-rich, of a rich country, not the rich of a poor one. Their duty to society is not by any means ignored; they do not salve their own consciences with a temple stuck with pieces of colored glass. They give to causes they respect, and many of them give a great deal. And they don't put on a feast like this because they want to show off, or even because they are themselves gluttonous. They do it because they think their guests will enjoy it; they do it to introduce a struggling young artist. And anyway, why should good eating be immoral?

You pay nothing for it, Murthi says. It is too easy. It does not come after hard times and starvation, but after plenty. It is nothing but self-indulgence. It smothers the spiritual life. In the midst of plenty, that is the time to fast.

I am too full to argue with him. I feel as if I might lift into the air and float away, and the whole unreal patio with me, bearing its umbrella of artificial moonlight and its tables and people and glass-fronted cabaña, its piano and its Artist, high above the crass valley. It is like a New Yorker cartoon, and me with my turned-up Muslim slippers and baggy pants, one of the Peninsula pashas on a magic carpet of the latest model, complete with indirect lighting, swimming pool, Muzak, and all modern conveniences.

All? Nothing forgotten? My feet insist on my notice. I stoop on the sly and feel the cement. Sure enough, the magic carpet has radiant heating too.

v

Kaminski is booted and spurred and ready to ride. The audience is braced between the cabaña and the pool. The moonlight is turned off. The air is cool and damp, but the pavement underfoot radiates its faint expensive warmth. Inside, one light above the piano shines on Kaminski's white jacket as he sits fiddling with the knobs, adjusting the bench. The shadow of the piano's open wing falls across his head. The Degas has become a Rembrandt.

On a lounge sofa between Sue and Ruth, old Joe Allston, very much overfed, is borne up like a fly on meringue. Bill has creaked away somewhere. A partition has slid across the barbecue, and from behind it, during pauses in the hum of talk, comes the sound of a busy electric dishwater.

"Are people too comfortable, do you think?" Sue asks. "Would it have been better to put out undertaker's chairs?"

I assure her that she has the gratitude of every over-burdened pelvis in the house. "There is no such thing as too comfortable," I say, "any more than there is such a thing as a large drink of whiskey."

Her hands pick at things on her dress and are held still. Her laugh fades away in a giggle.

I say, "What's he going to play?" and quite loudly she bursts out, "I don't know! He wouldn't tell me!" One or two shadowy heads turn. Kaminski stares out into the dusk from his bench, and the shadow wipes all the features off his face.

We are sitting well back, close to the edge of the pool. "How did you manage to get him to play after all?" Ruth murmurs.

It is as improbable to see the sneering curl of Sue's lip as it would be to see an ugly scowl on her face. "I *crawled!*" she says.

The cushions sigh as Ruth eases back into them. But I am sitting where I can watch Sue's face, and I am not so easily satisfied. "Why?" I ask.

"Because he's a great artist."

"Oh." After a moment I let myself back among the cushions with Ruth. "I hope he is," I say, and at least for the moment I mean it.

The eyeless mask of Kaminski's face turns again. Even when he speaks he does not seem to have lips. "For my first number I play three Chopin Nocturnes. I play these as suitable to the occasion, and especially for Mrs. Casement."

Beside me I can feel Sue shrink. I have a feeling, though it is too dark to see, that she has flushed red. While the murmur rising from the audience says How nice, handsome gesture, what a nice compliment, she looks at her hands.

At the piano, Kaminski kneads his knuckles, staring at the empty music rack. When he has held his pose of communing with his *Geist* long enough for the silence to spread to the far edges of the audience, but not long enough so that any barbarian starts talking again, he drops into the music with a little skip and a trill. It is well timed and well executed. Without knowing it, probably, Sue takes hold of my hand. She is like a high school girl who shuts her eyes while the hero plunges from the two-yard line. Did he make it? Oh, did he go over?

The cabaña acts like a shell; the slightest pianissimo comes out feathery but clear, and Kaminski's meaty hands are very deft. Behind us the faint gurgle and suck of the pool's filter system is a watery night-sound under the Chopin.

God spare me from ever being called a critic or even a judge of music — even a listener. Like most people, I think I can tell a dub from a competent hand, and it is plain at once that Kaminski is competent. The shades of competence are another thing. They are where the Soul

comes in, and I look with suspicion on those who wear
their souls outside. I am not capable in any case of judging
Kaminski's soul. Maybe it is such a soul as swoons into the
world only once in a hundred years. Maybe, again, it is
such a G.G. soul as I have seen on Madison Avenue and
elsewhere in my time.

But I think I can smell a rat, even in music, if it is dead
enough, and as Kaminski finishes one nocturne and chills
into abashed silence those who have mistakenly started to
applaud too soon, and pounds into the second with big
chords, I think I begin to smell a rat here. Do I imagine it,
or is he burlesquing these nocturnes? Is he contemptuous
of them because they are sentimental, because they are
nineteenth century, because they don't strain his keyboard
technique enough, or because he knows Sue adores them?
And is he clever enough and dirty enough to dedicate them
to her as an insult?

It is hard to say. By the third one it is even harder, because he has played them all with great precision even
while he gives them a lot of bravura. I wish I could ask
Ruth what she thinks, because her ear for music and her
nose for rats are both better than mine. But there is no
chance, and so I am still nursing the private impression that
Kaminski is hoaxing the philistines when I am called on to
join in the applause, which is loud, long, and sincere. If
the philistines have been hoaxed, they are not aware of the
fact. Beside me, Sue wears her hands out; she is radiant.
"Oh, didn't he play them *beautifully?* They loved it, didn't
they? I told you, *nobody* can play Chopin the way Arnold
can."

In the second row of lounge chairs the musical crowd,
satisfactorily applauding, bend heads each to other. Mr.
Ackerman's big droopy face lifts solemnly against the light.

Kaminski, after his bow, has seated himself again and waits while the clapping splatters away and the talk dies down again and a plane, winking its red and white wing lights, drones on down and blinks out among the stars over Black Mountain. Finally he says, "I play next the Bach Chaconne, transcribed for piano by Busoni."

"What is it?" Sue says. "Should I know it?"

Over Sue's head Ruth gives me one of her raccoon looks. I am delighted; I rouse myself. This time my lie detector is going to be a little more searching, because I have heard a dozen great pianists play the Chaconne, and I own every recording ever made, probably. Every time I catch a competent amateur at a piano I beg it out of him. In my opinion, which I have already disparaged, it is only the greatest piece of music ever written, a great big massive controlled piece of mind. If Kaminski can play the Chaconne and play it well, I will forgive him and his bad manners and his tantrums and the Polish soul he put into Chopin. It takes more than Polish soul to play the Chaconne. It takes everything a good man has, and a lot of good men don't have enough.

Maybe Kaminski does have enough. He states those big sober themes, as they say in music-appreciation circles, with, as they also say, authority. The great chords begin to pile up. Imagine anyone writing that thing in the first place for the violin. As usual, it begins to destroy me. Kaminski is great, he's tremendous, he is tearing into this and bringing it out by the double handful. A success, a triumph. Listen to it roll and pour, and not one trace, not a whisker, of Polish soul. This is the language you might use in justifying your life to God.

As when, in the San Francisco Cow Palace, loudspeakers announce the draft horse competition, and sixteen great

Percherons trot with high action and ponderous foot into the arena, brass-harnessed, plume-bridled, swelling with power, drawing the rumbling brewery wagon lightly, Regal Pale: ton-heavy but light-footed they come, the thud of their hoofs in the tanbark like the marching of platoons, and above them the driver spider-braced, intent, transmits through the fan of lines his slightest command: lightly he guides them, powerfully and surely they bring their proud necks, their plumed heads, their round and dappled haunches, the blue and gold wagon Regal Pale —sixteen prides guided by one will, sixteen great strengths respondent and united: so the great chords of Bach roll forth from under the hands of Arnold Kaminski.

And as, half trained or self-willed, the near leader may break, turn counter to his driver's command, and in an instant all that proud unanimity is a snarl of tangled traces and fouled lines and broken step and cross purposes and desperate remedies, so at a crucial instant fails the cunning of Kaminski. A butch, a fat, naked, staring discord.

To do him credit, he retrieves it instantly, it is past and perhaps not even noticed by many. But he has lost me, and when I have recovered from the momentary disappointment I am cynically amused. The boy took on something too big for him. A little later he almost gets me back, in that brief lyrical passage that is like a spring in a country of cliffs, but he never does quite recover the command he started with, and I know now how to take him.

When he finishes there is impressed silence, followed by loud admiration. This has been, after all — Allston *dicens* — the most magnificent piece of music ever written, and it ought to be applauded. But it has licked Kaminski in a spot or two, and he can't help knowing it and knowing that the musicians present know it. As he stands up to take a bow, his face, thrust up into the light, acquires features, a mask of slashes and slots and knobs, greenish and shadowed. He looks like a rather bruised corpse, and he bows as if greeting his worst enemy. In the quiet as the applause finally dies out I hear the gurgle of the pool's drain and catch a thin aseptic whiff of chlorine, a counter-whiff of cigar smoke and perfume.

Says Sue in my ear, tensely, "What did I tell you?"

"For my last number," Kaminski's thick voice is saying, "I play the Piano Pieces of Arnold Schoenberg, Opus 19."

I have had Schoenberg and his followers explained to me, even urged upon me, several times, generally by arty people who catch me with my flank exposed at a cocktail party. They tell me that these noises are supposed, among other things, to produce *tension*. Tension is a great word among the tone-row musicians. God bless them, they are good at it. It astonishes me anew, as Kaminski begins, that sounds like these can come out of a piano. They can only be recovered from through bed rest and steam baths, maybe shock therapy.

For no amount of argument can convince me that this music does not hurt the ears. And though I am prepared to admit that by long listening a man might accustom himself to it, I do not think this proves much. Human beings can adjust to anything, practically; it is a resilient race. We can put up with the rule of kings, presidents, priests, dictators, generals, communes, and committees; we learn to tolerate diets of raw fish, octopus, snails, unborn ducklings, clay, the bleeding hearts of enemies, our own dung; we learn to listen without screaming to the sounds of samisens, Korean harps, veenas, steam whistles, gongs, and Calypso singers; we adjust bravely to whole-tone, half-tone, or quarter-tone scales, to long skirts and short skirts, crew cuts and perukes, muttonchops and dundrearies and Van Dykes and naked chins, castles and paper houses and *barastis* and bomb shelters. The survival of the race depends upon its infinite adaptability. We can get used to anything in time, and even perhaps develop a perverted taste for it. But *why?* The day has not come when I choose to try adapting to Schoenberg. Schoenberg hurts my ears.

He hurts some other ears, too. The audience that has swooned at the Chopin and been respectful before the Bach is systematically cut to ribbons by the saw edges of the Piano Pieces. I begin to wonder all over again if Kaminski may have planned this program with perverse cunning: throw the philistines the Chopin, giving it all the *Schmalz* it will stand; then stun them with the Bach (only the Bach was too much for him); then trample them contemptuously underfoot with the Schoenberg, trusting that their ignorance will be impressed by this wrenched and tortured din even while they writhe under it. A good joke. But then what is he after? It is his own career that is at stake, he is the one who stands to benefit if the musicians' corner is impressed. Does he mean to say the hell with it on these terms, or am I reading into a not-quite-good-enough pianist a lot of ambiguities that don't exist in him?

It slowly dawns on me, while I grit my teeth to keep from howling like a dog, that Kaminski *means* this Schoenberg. He gives it the full treatment; he visibly wrestles with the Ineffable. Impossible to tell whether he hits the right notes or the wrong ones — probably Schoenberg himself couldn't tell. Wrong ones better, maybe — more tension. But Kaminski is concentrating as if the music ties him into bundles of raw nerves. For perhaps a second there is a blessed relief, a little thread of something almost a melody, and then the catfight again. Language of expressionism, tension and space, yes. Put yourself in the thumbscrew and any sort of release is blessed. Suite for nutmeg grater, cactus, and strings. A garland of loose ends.

He is putting himself into it devotionally; he *is* Schoenberg. I recall a picture of the composer on some record envelope — intense staring eyes, bald crown, temples with a cameo of raised veins, cheeks bitten in, mouth grim and bitter, unbearable pain. Arnold Schoenberg, Destroyer and Preserver. Mouthful of fire and can neither swallow nor spit.

In the cone of light under which Kaminski tortures himself and us, I see a bright quick drop fall from the end of his nose. Sweat or hay fever? Soul or allergy? Whatever it is, no one can say he isn't trying.

The piano stops with a noise like a hiccup or a death rattle. Three or four people laugh. Kaminski sits still. The audience waits, not to be caught offside. This might be merely space, there might be some more tension coming. But Kaminski is definitely through. Applause begins, with the overenthusiastic sound of duty in it, and it dies quickly except in the musical row, where the accompanist is clapping persistently.

Sue is clapping her hands in intense slow strokes under her chin. "Isn't that something?" she says. "That's one thing he's been working on a lot. I just don't see how anybody plays it at all — all those minor ninths and major sevenths, and no key signature at all."

"Or *why* anybody plays it," I am compelled to say. But when her hands start another flurry I join in. Kaminski sits, spiritually exhausted, bending his head. Encore, encore. For Sue's sake, try. My arms begin to grow tired, and still he sits there. A full minute after my impertinent question, her hands still going, Sue says, "I admit *I* don't understand that kind of music, but because I'm ignorant is no reason to throw it away."

So I am rebuked. She is a noble and innocent woman, and will stoop to beg Kaminski and leave a door open for Schoenberg, all for the disinterested love of art. Well, God bless her. It's almost over, and she can probably feel that it was a success. Maybe she can even think of it as a triumph. Later, when nothing has come of all her effort and expense, she can console herself with a belief that there is a conspiracy among established musicians to pound the fingers of drowning genius off the gunwale.

"Well, anyway, *he's* terrific," I say like a forktongued liar. "Marvelous." Rewarded by all the gratitude she puts into her smile, I sit back for the encore that is finally forth-coming. And what does Kaminski play? Some number of Charles Ives, almost as mad as the Schoenberg.

Probably there might have been enough politeness among us to urge a second encore, but Kaminski cuts us off by leaving the piano. Matches flare, smoke drifts up-ward, the moonlight dawns again, Bill Casement appears from somewhere, and a discreet white coat crosses from the barbecue end of the cabaña and opens the folding panels of the bar.

VI

It seems that quite a number of times during the evening I am condemned to have Sue at me with tense questions. She is as bad as a Princeton boy with a manuscript: *Have I got it? Is it any good? Can I be a writer?* "What do you think?" Sue says now. "Am I wrong?"

"He's a good pianist."

Her impatience is close to magnificent. For a second

she is Tallulah. "Good! Good heavens, I know that. But does he have a chance? Has he got so much talent they can't deny him? They say only about one young pianist in a hundred . . ."

"You can't make your chances," I say. "That's mostly luck."

"I'll be his luck," she says.

The crowd is rising and drifting inside. Trapped on the lounge, I lean back and notice that over our heads, marbled by the lights, white mist has begun to boil on some unfelt wind. The air is chilly and wet; the fog has come in. Ruth stands up, shivering her shoulders to cover the significant look she is giving me. I stand up with her. So does Sue, but Sue doesn't let me go.

"If you're his luck, then he has a chance," I say, and am rewarded by one of her smiles, so confident and proud that I am stricken with remorse, and add, "But it's an awful skinny little chance. Any young pianist would probably be better off if he made up his mind straight off to be a local musician instead of trying for a concert career."

"But the concert career is what he wants. It's what he's been preparing for all his life."

"Sure. That's what they all want. Then they eat their hearts out because they miss, and when you look at it, what is it they've missed? A chance to ride a dreary circuit and play for the local Master Minds and Artists series and perform in the Art Barn of every jerk town in America. It might be better if they stayed home and organized chamber groups and taught the young and appeared once a year as soloist with the local little symphony."

"Joe, dear," Sue says, "can you imagine Arnold teaching grubby little unwilling kids to play little Mozart sonatas for PTA meetings?"

She could not have found a quicker way to adjust my thermostat upward. It is true that I can't imagine Kaminski doing any such thing as teaching the young, but that is a commentary on Kaminski, not on the young. Besides, I am the defender, self-appointed, of the good American middle class small-town and suburban way of life, and I get almighty sick of Americans who enjoy all its benefits but can't find a good word to say for it. An American may be defined as a man who won't take his own side in an argument. "Is Arnold *above* Mozart?" I ask. "For that matter, is he above the PTA?"

She stares at me to see if I'm serious. "Now you're being cute," she says, and blinks her eyes like a fond idiot and rushes inside to join the group around Kaminski. I note that Kaminski now has a highball in his hand. The Artist is only mortal, after all. If we wait, we may even see him condescend to a sandwich.

"Shall we get out of this?" I ask Ruth.

"Not yet."

"Why not?"

"Manners," she says. "You wouldn't understand, lamb. But let's go inside. It's cold out here."

It is, even with the radiant-heated magic carpet. The patio is deserted already. The air above boils with white. Between the abandoned chairs and empty lawn the transparent green-blue pool fumes with underwater light as if it opened down into hell. Once inside and looking out, I have a feeling of being marooned in a space ship. Any minute now frogmen will land their saucers on the patio or rise in diving helmets and snorkels from the pool.

Inside there are no frogmen, only Kaminski, talking with his hands, putting his glass on a tray and accepting another.

The white head of the critic is humorously and skeptically bent, listening. The dour accompanist, the velvet-coated Mr. Budapest, the solid Ackermans, Sue, three or four unknowns, the little piano teacher, make a close and voluble group. Kaminski pauses amid laughter; evidently these others don't find him as hard to take as I do. As if he feels my thoughts, he looks across his hearers at Ruth and me, and Ruth raises her hands beside her head and makes pretty applauding motions. Manners. I am compelled to do the same, not so prettily.

Sam Shields goes past us, winks sadly, leaving. His wife is crippled and does not go out, so that he is always among the first to leave a party. This time he has five or six others for company, filing past Bill and being handshook at the door. To us now comes Annie Williamson, robust dame, and inquires in her fight-announcer's voice why we don't join the Hunt. They have fourteen members now, and enough permissions so that they can put hurdles on fences and get a run of almost fourteen miles. Of course we're not too old. Come on . . . Herman Dyer will still take a three-bar gate, and he's five years older than God. Or maybe we'd like the job of riding ahead dragging a scent or a dead rabbit. Make me Master of the Hunt, any office I want. Only come.

"Annie," I tell her sadly, "I am an old, infirm, pathetic figure. I have retired to these hills only to complete my memoirs, and riding a horse might cut them untimely short. Even art, such as tonight, can hardly make me leave my own humble hearth any more."

"What's the matter?" she says. "Didn't you like it? I thought it was swell. The last one was kind of yowly, but he played it fine."

"Sure I liked it," I say. "I thought it was real artistic."

"You're a philistine," Annie says. "An old cynical philistine. I'd hate to read your memoirs."

"You couldn't finish them," I say. "There isn't a horse or a beagle in them anywhere."

"A terribly limited old man," she says, and squeezes Ruth's arm and goes off shaking her head and chuckling. She circles the Kaminski crowd, interrupts something he is saying. I see her mouth going: Thank you, enjoyed it very much, blah blah. She first, and now a dozen others, neighbors and unknowns . . . so much . . . envy Sue the chance to hear you every day . . . luck to you . . . great treat. Some more effusive than others, but all respectful. Kaminski can sneer at his overfed alcoholic audience, but it has listened dutifully, and has applauded louder than it sometimes felt like doing, and has stilled its laughter in embarrassment when it didn't understand. If he had played nothing but Chopin they would have enjoyed him more, but he would have to be even more arrogant and superior and crossgrained than he is to alienate their good will and sour their wonderful good nature. Luck to you . . . And mean it. Would buy tickets, if necessary.

"Madame," I say to my noiseless wife, "art is troublesome and life is long. Can't we go home?"

For answer she steers me by the arm into the musical circle. Except for four people talking over something confidential in a corner, and the white coats moving around hopefully with unclaimed highballs on their trays, the musical circle now includes the whole company. Kaminski, we find, is still doing most of the talking. His subject is — guess what? The Artist. Specifically, the Artist in America.

I claim one of the spare highballs in self-defense. I know

the substance of this lecture in advance, much of it from Murthi. And if Kaminski quotes Baudelaire about the great gaslighted Barbarity that killed Poe, I will disembowel him.

The lecture does not pursue its expected course more than a few minutes, and it is done with more grace and humor than I would have thought Kaminski had in him. A couple of highballs have humanized his soul. Mainly he talks, and without too obvious self-pity, about the difficulties of a musical career: twenty years or so of nothing but practice, practice, practice; the teachers in Boston and New York and Rome; the tyranny of the piano (I can't be away from a piano a single day without losing ground. On the train, and even in an automobile, I carry around a practice keyboard to run exercises on). It is (with a rueful mouth) a rough profession to get established in. He wonders sometimes why one doesn't instead take the Civil Service examinations. (Laughter.) But it is understandable, Kaminski says, why the trapdoor should be closed over the heads of young musicians. Established performers, and recording companies and agencies clinging to what they know is profitable, are naturally either jealous of competition or afraid to risk anything on new music or new men. (That charming little Ives that I used for an encore, for instance, has practically never been played, though it was composed almost fifty years ago.)

The case of Kaminski is (with a shrug) nothing unique. The critic and the Ackermans know how it goes. And of course, there is the problem of finding audiences. Whom shall one play for? Good audiences so few and so small, in spite of all the talk about the educational effect of radio and recordings. People who really know and love good music available only in the large cities or — with a flick of his dark eyes at Sue — in a few places such as this. Oh, he is full of charm. The little music teacher bridles. But generally, Kaminski says, there is only the sham audience with sham values, and the whole concert stage which is the only certain way of reaching the audiences one can respect is dominated by two or three agencies interested only in dollars.

"Shyme, shyme," says old Joe Allston from the edge of the circle, and draws a startled half-smile from his neighbors and a second's ironic stare from Kaminski.

"What, a defender of agents in the crowd?" the critic says, turning his white head.

"Literary only," I say. "And ex, not current. But a bona fide paid-up member of the Agents' Protective Association, the only bulwark between the Artist and the poor farm."

"Are agents so necessary?" Sue says. "Isn't it possible to break in somehow without putting yourself in the clutches of one of them?"

"Clutches!" I say. "Consider my feelings."

Ruth gives me an absolutely expressionless, pleasant look in which I read some future unpleasantness, but what the hell, shall a man keep quiet while his lifework is trampled on?

"Would you admit," says Kaminski with his tight dogfish smile, "that an agent without an artist is a vine without an oak?"

The little music teacher brings her hands together. Her eyes are snapping and her little pointed chin, pebbled like the Pope's Nose of a plucked turkey, quivers. Oh, if she were defending the cause of music and art against such commercial attacks, she would . . . She is listening, comprehending, participating, right in the midst of things. Kaminski turns to her and actually winks. As a tray passes behind him he reaches back and takes a third highball. Joe Allston collars one too. The benevolent critic pokes his finger at old Joe and says encouragingly, "How about it, Agents' Protective Association? Can you stand alone?"

"I don't like the figure," I say. "I don't feel like a vine without an oak. I feel like a Seeing Eye dog without a blind man."

This brings on a shower of protests and laughter, and Sue says, "Joe, if you're going to stick up for agents you'll have to tell us how to beat the game. How could an agent help Arnold, say, get a hearing and get started?"

"Any good agency will get him an audition, any time."

"Yes, along with a thousand others."

"No, by himself."

"And having had it, what does he get out of it?" murmurs Mr. Ackerman. He has winesap cheeks and white, white hair, but his expression is not benevolent like the critic's, mainly because his whole face has come loose, and sags — big loose lips, big drooping nose, a forehead that hangs in folds over his eyebrows. He reminds me of a worried little science-fiction writer I used to know who developed what his doctor called "lack of muscle tone," so that his nose wouldn't even hold up his glasses. It was as if he had been half disintegrated by one of his ray guns. Mr. Ackerman's voice sags like his face; he looks at me with reddish eyes above hound-dog lower lids.

They all obviously enjoy yapping at me. Here is the Enemy, the Commercial Evil Genius that destroys Art. This kind of thing exhilarates me, I'm afraid.

"That's not the agent's fault," I say. "It's a simple matter of supply and demand. A hundred good young pianists come to New York every year all pumped full of hope. They are courteously greeted and auditioned by the agents, who take on anyone they can. Agents arrange concerts, including Town Hall and Carnegie Hall concerts, for some of them, and they paper the hall and invite and inveigle the critics and clip the reviews, and if the miracle happens and some young man gets noticed in some special way, they book him on a circuit. But if ninety-nine of those young pianists slink out of New York with a few pallid clippings and no rave notices and no bookings, that isn't the agents' fault."

"Then whose fault is it?" cries Sue. "There are millions of people who would be thrilled to hear someone like Arnold play. Why can't they? There seems to be a stone wall between."

"Overproduction," murmurs old Devil's-Advocate Allston, and sips his insolent bourbon.

Mr. Ackerman's face lifts with a visible effort its sagging folds; the critic looks ironical and skeptical; Kaminski watches me over his glass with big shining liquid eyes. His pitted skin is no longer pale, but has acquired a dark, purplish flush. He seems to nurse some secret amusing knowledge. The music teacher at his elbow twists her mouth, very incensed and impatient at old commercial Allston. Her mouth opens for impetuous words, closes again. Her pebbled chin quivers.

"Overproduction, sure," I say again. "If it happened in the automobile industry you'd blame it on the management, or the government, or on classical capitalist economics, or creeping socialism. But it's in music, and so you want to blame it on the poor agent. An agent is only a dealer. He isn't to blame if the factory makes too many cars. All he can do is sell the ones he can."

"I'm afraid Mr. Allston is pulling our leg," the critic says.

"Art isn't quite a matter of production lines. Genius can't be predicted and machined like a Chevrolet, do you think, Mr. Casement?"

He catches Bill by surprise. Evidently he is one of those who like to direct and control conversations, pulling in the hangers-on. But his question is no kindness to Bill, who strangles and waves an arm. "Don't ask me! I don't know a thing about it." Even after the spotlight has left him, he stands pulling his lower lip, looking around over his hand, and chuckling meaninglessly when he catches anyone's eye.

"So you don't think a New York concert does any good," Sue says — pushing, pushing. After all, she held this clambake to bring us all together and now she has what she wanted — patrons and critics and agents in a cluster — and she is going to find out everything. "If they don't do any good, why bother?"

"Why indeed," I say, and then I see that I have carried it too far, for Sue's face puckers unhappily, and she insists, "But Joe . . ."

The critic observes, "They may not do much good, but nothing can be done *without* one."

"So for the exceptional ones they *do* do some good."

"For the occasional exception they may do everything," the critic says. "Someone like William Kapell, who was killed in a plane crash just a few miles from here. But Kapell was a *very* notable exception."

I cannot read Kaminski — it is being made increasingly clear to me that one of my causes of irritation at him is precisely that I don't know what goes on inside him — but I can read Sue Casement without bifocals, and the look she throws at Kaminski says two things: One is that here, just five feet from her, is another Notable Exception as notable as Kapell. The other is that since Kapell has been killed on the brink of a brilliant career, he has obviously left a vacancy.

"A lot of young pianists can't afford it, I expect," she says — hopefully, I think.

The critic spreads his hands. "Town Hall about fifteen hundred, Carnegie two thousand. Still, a lot of them find it somewhere. It's a lot of money to put on the turn of a card."

Determination and resolve, or muscular contractions that I interpret in these terms, harden in Sue's rosy face. "Is it hard to arrange?"

I can't resist. "Any good agent will take care of it for you," I say. She throws me a smile: you old devil, you.

"But no one can count on one single thing's coming from it," the critic says, and he looks kindly upon both Sue and her protégé. I respect this benevolent old creature in spite of his profession. He is trying to warn them.

Not being one of these socially clairvoyant people, I would not feel extraordinarily at home in a Virginia Woolf novel. But I get a glimpse, for the most fragmentary moment, of an extreme complexity pressing in upon us. There is of course Ruth emanating silent disapproval of her husband's big argumentative mouth, and there is Sue, radiant and resolute, smiling promises at Kaminski. There is Kaminski with his deer eyes wide and innocent, his mouth indifferently half smiling — a pure enigma to me, unidentifiable. And there are the critic, ruminating kindly and perhaps with friendly sorrow his own private doubts, and Ackerman incognito behind the heavy folds of his face, and Mrs. Ackerman who looks as if she would like nothing better than to get off her aching feet and start home, and the music teacher bristling with excitement and stimulation, saying to Kaminski, "But *imagine* getting up on the stage at Carnegie Hall with Virgil Thompson and Olin Downes and everybody there . . ." Also there is Bill Casement with his long creased face that looks as overworked as Gary Cooper trying to register an emotion. What emotion? Maybe he is kissing two thousand dollars goodbye and wondering if he is glad to see it go. Maybe he is proud of his wife, who has the initiative and the culture to do all this of this evening. Maybe he is contemplating the people in his cabaña and thinking what funny things can happen to a man's home.

So only one thing is clear. Sue will stake Kaminski to a New York concert. I don't know why that depresses me. It has been clear all along that that is exactly what she has wanted to do. My depression may come from Kaminski's indifference. I would like to see the stinker get his chance and goof it good.

An improbable opening appears low down in the droops and folds of Mr. Ackerman's face, and he yawns. "Darling," his wife says at once, "we have a long drive back to the city."

In a moment the circle has begun to melt and disintegrate. Sue is accosted with gratitude from three sides. The accompanist and the velvet-coated Mr. Budapest stay with Kaminski to say earnest friendly things: I want you to come up and meet . . . He will be interested that you have appeared with . . . of course they will have heard of you . . . I should think something of Hovhaness' . . . yes . . . excellent. Why not?

Since the discussion took his career out of his hands, Kaminski has said nothing. He bows, he smiles, but his face has gone remote; the half-sneer of repose has come back into it. He is a Hyperborean, beyond everybody. All this nonsense about careers bores him. Why do the heathen rage furiously together? Beyond question, he is one of the greatest bargains I have ever seen bought.

Also, as he turns and shakes hands with Mr. Budapest and recalls himself for the tiresomeness of goodnights, I observe that perhaps what I took for snootiness is paralysis. He does not believe in alcohol, which is drunk only by pigs, but I have seen him take four highballs in twenty minutes, and Bill Casement's bartenders have been taught not to spare the Old Granddad.

VII

While the other ladies are absent getting their coats, Kaminski holds collapse off at arm's length and plays games of solemn jocularity with the homely little music teacher. He leans carefully and whispers in her ear something that makes her flush and laugh and shake her head, protesting. "Eh?" he cries. "Isn't it so?" With his feet crossed he leans close, rocking his ankles. Out of the corner of the music teacher's eye goes an astonishingly cool flickering look, alert to see if anyone is watching her here, tête-a-tête with the maestro. All she sees is old Joe Allston, the commercial fellow. Her neck stiffens, her eyes are abruptly glazed, her face is carefree and without guile as she turns indifferently back. Old Allston is about as popular as limburger on the newlyweds' exhaust manifold. He hates us Youth. The Anti-Christ.

"You can joke," she says to Kaminski, "but I'm serious,

really I am. We know we aren't very wonderful, but we aren't so bad, either, so there. We've got a very original name: The Chamber Society. And if you don't watch out, I *will* sign you up to play with us sometime. So don't say anything you don't mean!"

"I never say anything I don't mean," Kaminski grins. "I'd love to play with you. All ladies, are you?"

"All except the cello. He's a math teacher at the high school."

"Repulsive," Kaminski murmurs. The teacher giggles, swings sideways, sees me still there, nails me to the wall with a venomous look. Snoop! Why don't I move? But I am much too interested to move.

"Three ladies and one gentleman," Kaminski says, smiling broadly and leaning over her so far he overbalances and staggers. "A Mormon. Are the other ladies all like you?"

Because I know that none of this will sound credible when I report it to Ruth, I strain for every word of this adolescent drooling. I see the music teacher, a little hesitant, vibrate a look at Kaminski's face and then, just a little desperately, toward the group of men by the door. Kaminski is greatly amused by something. "I tell you what you should do," he says. "You reorganize yourself into the Bed-chamber Society. Let the Mormon have the other two, and you and I will play together. Any time."

He has enunciated this unkind crudity very plainly, so plainly that at fifteen feet I cannot possibly have misheard. The little teacher does not look up from her abstract or panicky study of certain chair legs. Her incomplete little face goes slowly scarlet, her pebbled chin is stiff. That little cold venomous glance whips up to me and is taken back again. If I were not there, she would probably run for her life. As it is, she is tempted into pretending that nothing has been said. She is like Harold Lloyd in one of those old comedies, making vivacious and desperate chatter to a girl, while behind the draperies or under the tablecloth his accidentally snagged pants unravel or his seams burst or his buttons one by one give up the ghost. Sooner or later the draperies will be thrown open by the butler, or someone's belt buckle will catch the tablecloth and drag it to the floor, and there will be Harold in his hairy shanks, his Paris garters. Oh Lord. I am not quite able to take myself away from there.

Kaminski leans over her, catches himself by putting a hand on her shoulder, says something else close to her red-hot ear. That does it. She squirms sideways, shakes him off, and darts past the ladies just returning from the cloak-room. Kaminski, not so egg-eyed as I expect to see him, looks at me with a smile almost too wide for his mouth, and winks. He could not be more pleased if he had just pulled the legs off a live squirrel. But the music teacher, darting past me, has given me quite another sort of look. There is a dead-white spot in the center of each cheek, and her eyes burn into mine with pure hatred. That is what I get for being an innocent bystander and witnessing her humiliation.

For a few seconds Kaminski stands ironically smiling into thin air; he wears a tasting expression. Then he motions to one of the Japanese at the bar, and the Japanese scoops ice cubes into a glass.

It is time for us to get away from there. The elegant cabaña smells and looks like Ciro's at nine o'clock of a Sunday morning. Outside, the pool lights are off, but the air swirls and swims, dizzy with moonlighted fog. The sliding doors are part way open for departing guests. Sue comes and catches Kaminski by the arm, holding his sleeve with both hands in a too friendly, too sisterly pose. They stand in the doorway with the mist blowing beyond them.

"Now please do come and see me," Ackerman says. "One never knows. I would like to introduce you. Perhaps some evening, a little group at my home."

"Good luck," says the critic. "I shall hope before long to write pleasant comments after your name."

"Ah, vunderful," says Mr. Budapest, "you vere vunderful! I have so enjoyed it. And if you should write to Signor Vitelli, my greetings. It has been many years."

"Not at all, not at all," says Bill Casement. "Happy to have you."

"It was so good of you all to come," Sue says. "You don't know how . . . or rather, you do, all of you do. You've been generous to come and help. I'm sure it will work out for him somehow, he has such great talent. And when you're as ignorant as I am . . . I hope when you're down this way you won't hesitate . . . Goodbye, goodbye, goodbye."

The women pull June fur coats around them, their figures blur in the mist and are invisible beyond the Mondrian gate. But now comes the music teacher with a bone in her teeth, poor thing, grimly polite, breathless. She looks neither to left nor right past Sue's face: Goodnight. A pleasant time. You have a very beautiful place. Thank you. And gone.

Her haste is startling to Sue, who likes to linger warmly on farewells, standing with arms hugged around herself in lighted doorways. Kaminski toasts the departing tweed with a silent glass. The figure hurries through the gate, one shoulder thrust ahead, the coat thrown cape-wise over her shoulders. Almost she scuttles. From beyond the gate she casts back one terrible glance, and is swallowed in the fog.

"Why, I wonder what's the matter with her?" Sue says. "Didn't she act odd?"

Bill motions us in and slides the glass door shut. With his back against the door Kaminski studies the ice cubes which remain from his fifth highball. All of a sudden he is as gloomy as a raincloud. "I'm the matter with her," he says. "I insulted her."

"You *what?*"

"Insulted her. I made indecent propositions."

"Oh, Arnold!" Sue says with a laugh. "Come on!"

"It's true," Arnold says. "Ask the agent, there. I whispered four-letter words in her ear."

She stares at him steadily. "And if you did," she says, "in heaven's name *why* did you?"

"Akh!" Kaminski says. "Such a dried-up little old maid as that, so full of ignorance and enthusiasm. How could I avoid insulting her? She is the sort of person who invites indecent exposure." There is a moment of quiet in which we hear the sound of a car pulling out of the drive. "How could I help insulting her?" Kaminski shouts. "If I didn't insult people like that I couldn't keep my self-respect." Nobody replied to this. "That is why nobody likes me," he says, and looks around for a white coat but the white coats are all gone. Automatically Sue takes his empty glass from him.

Ruth says, quite loudly for her, "Sue, we must go. It was a lovely party. And Mr. Kaminski, I thought you played beautifully."

His flat stare challenges her. "I was terrible," he says. "Ackerman and those others will tell you. They are saying right now in their car how bad it was. The way I played, they will think I am fit for high school assemblies or Miss Spinster's chamber society. I am all finished around here. Nothing will come of any of this. I have muffed it again."

"Finished?" Sue cries. "Arnold, you've just begun."

"Finished," he says. "All done."

"Oh, what if you did insult Miss What's-her-name," Sue says. "You can go and apologize tomorrow. It's your playing that's important, and you played so beautifully . . ."

Bill Casement, by the door jamb, rubs one cheek, pulling his mouth down and then up again. He gives me a significant look; I half expect him to twirl a finger beside his head. "Well, goodnight," I say. "I'm tired, and I imagine you all are."

Bill slides the door open a couple of feet, but Sue pays no attention to me. She is staring angrily at Kaminski. "How can you *talk* that way? You did beautifully — ask anybody who heard you. This is only the first step, and you got by it just — just wonderfully! I told you I'd back you, and I will."

I have never observed anyone chewing his tongue, but that is what Kaminski is doing now, munching away, and his purple cheeks working. His face has begun to degenerate above the black and white formality of jacket and pleated shirt and rigid black tie. "You're incurably kind," he says thickly — whether in irony or not I can't tell. He spits out his tongue and says more plainly, "You like me, I know that. You're the only one. Nobody else. Nobody ever did. This is the way it was in Hollywood too. Did you know I was in Hollywood a while? I had a job playing for the soundtrack of a Charles Boyer movie. So what did I do? I quarreled with the director and he got somebody else."

With a resolute move, Ruth and I get out the door. Pinpricks of fog are in our faces. From inside, Sue says efficiently, "Arnold, you've had one too many. It was a great success, really it was."

"Every time, I fail," wails Kaminski. His Mephisto airs have been melted and dissolved away; he is just a sloppy drunk with a crying jag on. His eyes beg pity and his mouth is slack and his hands paw at Sue. She holds him off by one thick wrist. "Every time," he says, and his eyes are on her now with a sudden drunken alertness. "Every time. You know why? I *want* to fail. I work like a dog for twenty years so I'll have the supreme pleasure of failing. Never knew anybody like that, did you? I'm very cunning. I plan it in advance. I fool myself right up to the last minute, and then the time comes and I know how cunningly I've been planning it all the time. I've been a failure all my life."

I am inclined to agree with him, but I am old and tired and fed up. I would also bet that he is well on his way to being an alcoholic, this anti-food-and-drink Artist. He has the proper self-pity. If you don't feel sorry for yourself in something like this you can't justify the bottle that cures and damns you. This Kaminski is one of those who drink for the hangover; he sins for the sweet torture of self-blame and confession. A crying jag is as good a way of holding the stage as playing the piano or bad manners.

Now he is angry again. "Why should a man have to scramble and crawl for a chance to play the soundtrack in a Boyer picture? That is how the artist is appreciated in this country. He plays offstage while a ham actor fakes for the camera. Why should I put up with that? If I'm an artist, I'm an artist. I would rather play the organ in some neon cocktail bar than do this behind-the-scenes faking."

"Of course," Sue says. "And tomorrow we can talk about how you're going to go ahead and be the artist you want to be. You can have the career you want, if you're willing to work hard — oh, so hard! But you have to have *faith* in yourself, Arnold! You have to have confidence that nothing on earth can stop you, and then it can't."

"Faith," says Kaminski. "Confidence!" He weaves on his feet, and his head rolls, and for a second I hope he has passed out so we can tote him off to bed. But he gets himself straightened up and under control again, showing a degree of co-ordination that makes me wonder all anew whether he is really as drunk as he seems or if he is putting on some fantastic act.

And then I find him looking out the open door with his mouth set in a mean little line. "You don't like me," he says. "You disliked me the minute you met me, and you've been watching me all night. You want to know why?"

"Not particularly," I say. "You'd better get to bed, and in the morning we can all be friends again."

"You're no friend of mine," says Kaminski, and Sue exclaims, "Arnold!" but Kaminski wags his head and repeats, "No frien' of mine, and I'll tell you why. You saw I was a fake. Looked right through me, didn' you? Smart man, can't be fooled just because somebody can play the piano. When did you decide I wasn't a Pole, eh? Tell me tha'."

I lift my shoulders. But it is true, now that I have had my attention called to it, that the slight unplaceable accent that was present earlier in the evening is gone. Now, even drunk and chewing his tongue, he talks a good deal like . . .

"Well, what is the accent?" I ask. "South Boston?"

"See, wha' I tell you?" he cries, and swings on Sue so that she has to turn with him and brace herself to hold him up. Her face puckers with effort, or possibly disgust, and now for the first time she is looking at Bill as a wife looks toward her husband when she needs to be got out of trouble. "See?" Kaminski shouts. "Wasn't fooled. You all were, but he wasn'. Regnize Blue Hill Avenue in a minute."

Again he drags himself up straight, holding his meaty hand close below his nose and studying it. "I'm a Pole from Egypt," he says. "Suffered a lot, been through Hell, made me diff'cult and queer. Eh?" He swings his eye around us, this preposterous scene-stealer; he holds us with his glittering eye. "Le' me tell you. Never been near Egypt, don't even know where Poland is on the map. My mother was not made into soap; she runs a copper and brass shop down by the North Station. So you wonner why people detes' me. Know why? I'm a fake, isn't an hones' thing about me. You jus' le'me go to Hell my own way, I'm good at it. I can lie my way in, and if I want I can lie my way out again. And what do you think of that?"

Bill Casement is the most good-natured of men, soft with his wife and overgenerous with his friends and more tolerant of all sorts of difference, even Kaminski's sort, than you would expect. But I watch him now, while Kaminski is falling all over Sue, and Sue is making half-disgusted efforts to prop him up, and I realize that Bill did not make his money scuffing his feet and pulling his cheek in embarrassment at soirées. Underneath the good-natured husband is a man of force, and in about one more minute he is due to light on Kaminski like the hammer of God.

Even while I think it, Bill reaches over and yanks him up and holds him by one arm. "All right," he says. "Now you've spilled it all. Let's go to bed."

"You too," Kaminski says. "You all hate me. You'll all wash your hands of me now. Well, why not? That Carnegie Hall promise, that won't hold when you know what kin' of person I am, eh? You'll all turn into enemies now."

"Is that what you *want*, Arnold?" Sue says bitterly. She looks ready to burst into tears.

"Tol' you I wanted to fail," he says — and even now, so help me, even out of his sodden and doughy wreckage, there looks that bright, mean, calculating little gleam of intelligence.

Bill says, "The only enemy you've got around here is your own mouth."

"My God!" Kaminski cries loudly. Either the fog has condensed on his face or he is sweating. I remember the bright drop from his nose while he struggled with the Piano Pieces. "My God," he says again, almost wearily. He hangs, surprisingly frail, from Bill's clutch; it is easy to forget, looking at his too-big head and his meaty hands, that he is really scrawny. "I'll tell you something else," he says. "You don't know right now whether what I've tol' you is true or if it isn'. Not even the smart one there. You don't know but what I've been telling you all this for some crazy reason of my own. Why would I? Does it make sense?" He drops his voice and peers around, grinning. "Maybe he's crazy. C'est dérangé."

"Come on," Bill says. He lifts Kaminski and starts him along, but Kaminski kicks loose and staggers and almost falls among the chairs in the foggy patio, and now what has been impossible becomes outrageous, becomes a vulgar burlesque — and I use the word vulgar deliberately, knowing who it is that speaks.

"Don't you worry about me!" Kaminski shouts, and kicks a chair over. "Don't you worry about a starving kike pianist from Blue Hill Avenue. Maybe I grew up in Egypt and maybe I didn't, but I can still play the piano. I can play the God damn keys off a piano."

He comes back closer, facing Sue with a chairback in his hands, bracing himself on it. "Don't worry," he says. "I can see you worrying, but don't worry. I'll be out of your damned little gardener's cottage in the morning, and thank you very much for nothing. Will that satisfy you?" With a jerk he throws the chair aside and it falls and clatters.

Bill Casement takes one step in Kaminski's direction, and the outrageous turns instantly into slapstick. The pianist squeaks like a mouse, turns and runs for his life. Behind a remoter chair he stops to show his teeth, but when Bill starts for him again he turns once more and runs. For a moment he hangs in mid-air, his legs going like a cat's held over water, and then he is in the pool. The splash comes up ghostly into the moonlight and the fog, and falls back again.

Maybe he can't swim. Maybe in his squeaking terror of what he has stirred up he has forgotten that the pool is there. Maybe he is so far gone that he doesn't even know he has fallen in. And maybe, on the other hand, he literally intends to drown himself.

If he does, he successfully fails in that too. By the time Bill has run to flip on the underwater lights the white coat is down under, and Kaminski is not struggling at all. While the women scream, Bill jumps into the water, and here he comes wading toward the shallow end dragging Kaminski under his arm. He hauls him up the corner steps and dangles him, shaking the water out of him, and Kaminski's arms drag on the tile and his feet hang limp.

"Oh my God," Sue whispers, "is he dead?"

Bill looks disgusted. After all, Kaminski couldn't have been in the pool more than a minute altogether. As Bill lowers him onto the warm pavement and straightens him out with his face turned sideways on his arm, Kaminski shudders and coughs. His hands make tense, meaty grabs at the concrete. The majordomo, Jerry, pops out of the kitchen end of the cabaña in his undershirt, takes one look, and pops back in again. In a moment he comes running with a blanket.

Kaminski is not seriously in need of a blanket. For the first time that evening, he is not seriously in need of an audience, either. We stay only long enough to see that Bill and Jerry have everything under control, and then we get away. Sue walks us to the gate, but it is impossible to say anything to her. She looks at us once so hurt and humiliated and ashamed that I feel like going back and strangling Kaminski for keeps where he lies gagging on the patio floor, and then we are alone in the surrealist fog-swept spaces of the parking area. In the car we sit for a minute or two letting the motor warm, while the windshield wipers make half-circles of clarity on the glass.

"I wonder what . . . " Ruth begins, but I put my hand over her mouth.

"Please. I am an old tired philistine who has had all he can stand. Don't even speculate on what's biting him, or why he acts the way he does. I've already given him more attention than I can justify."

As soon as I take my hand away, Ruth says softly, "The horrible part is, he played awfully well."

We are moving now out the fog-shrouded drive between curving rows of young pines. "What?" I say. "Did you think so?"

"Oh yes. Didn't you?"

"He hit a big blooper in the chaconne."

"That could happen to anybody, especially somebody young and nervous. But the interpretation — didn't you hear how he put himself into first the one and then the other, and how the whole quality changed, and how really authoritative he was in all of them? Some pianists can only play Mozart, or Beethoven, or Brahms. He can play anybody, and play him well. That's what Mr. Arpad said, too."

"Who's Mr. Arpad?"

"The one that accompanies singers."

"He thought he was good?"

"He told me he had come down expecting only another pianist, but he thought Kaminski had a real chance."

Tall eucalyptus trees are suddenly ghostly upreaching, the lights shine on their naked white trunks, the rails of a fence. I ease around a turn in second gear. "Well, all right," I say in intense irritation. "All right, he was good. But then why in the hell would he . . ."

And there we are back on it. Why would he? What made him? Was he lying at first, lying later, or lying all the time? And what is more important to me just then, where in God's name does he belong? What can the Sue Casements do for the Arnold Kaminskis, and where do the Bills come in, and what function, if any, is served by the contented, beagle-running, rabbit-chasing, patio-building, barbecuing exurbanites on their hundred hills? How shall a nest of robins deal with a cuckoo chick? And how should a cuckoo chick, which has no natural home except the one he usurps, behave himself in a robin's nest? And what if the cuckoo is sensitive, or Spiritual, or insecure? Christ.

Lights come at us, at first dim and then furry and enormous, the car behind them vaguely half seen, glimpsed and gone, and then the seethe of white again. I never saw the fog thicker; the whole cloudy blanket of the Pacific has poured over the Coast Range and blotted us out. I creep at ten miles an hour, peering for the proper turnoff on these unmarked country lanes.

The bridge planks rumble under us as I grope into our own lane. Half a mile more. Up there, the house will be staring blindly into cottonwool; my study below the terrace will be swallowed in fog; the oak tree where I do my birdwatching will have no limbs, no shade, no birds. Leaning to see beyond the switching wiper blades, I start up the last steep pitch, past the glaring-white gate, and on, tilting steeply, with the brown bank just off one fender and the gully's treetops fingering the fog like seaweed on the left. All blind, all difficult and blind. I taste the stale bourbon in my mouth and know myself for a frivolous old man.

In the morning, probably, the unidentifiable bird, towhee or whatever he is, will come around for another bout against the plate glass, hypnotized by the insane hostility of his double. I tell myself that if he wakes me again at dawn tomorrow with his flapping and pecking I will borrow a shotgun and scatter his feathers over my whole six acres.

Of course I will not. I know what I will do. I will watch the fool thing as long as I can stand it, and ruminate on the insanities of men and birds, and try to convince myself that as a local idiocy, an individual aberration, this behavior is not significant. And then when I cannot put up with the sight of this towhee any longer I will retire to my study and sit looking out the window into the quiet shade of the oak, where nuthatches are brownly and pertly content with the bugs in their home bark. But even down there I may sometimes hear the banging and thrashing of this dismal towhee trying to fight his way past himself into the living room of the main house.

We coast into the garage, come to a cushioned stop, look at each other.

"Tired?" Ruth whispers.

Her pert coon face glimmers in the dim light of the dash. Her eyes seem to be searching mine with a kind of anxiety. I notice that tired lines are showing around her mouth and eyes, and I am filled with gratitude for the forty years during which she has stood between me and myself.

"I don't know," I say, and kiss her and lean back. "I don't know whether I'm tired, or sad, or confused. Or maybe just irritated that they don't give you enough time in a single life to figure anything out."

the  traveler

HE WAS rolling in the first early dark down a snowy road, his headlights pinched between dark walls of trees, when the engine coughed, recovered, coughed again, and died. Down a slight hill he coasted in compression, working the choke, but at the bottom he had to pull over against the three-foot wall of plowed snow. Snow creaked under the tires as the car eased to a stop. The heater fan unwound with a final tinny sigh.

Here in its middle age this hitherto dependable mechanism had betrayed him, but he refused to admit immediately that he was betrayed. Some speck of dirt or bubble of water in the gas line, some momentary short circuit, some splash of snow on distributor points or plug connections — something that would cure itself before long. But turning off the lights and pressing on the starter brought no result; he held the choke out for several seconds, and got only the hopeful stink of gasoline; he waited and let the flooded carburetor rest and tried again, and nothing.

Eventually he opened the door and stepped out onto the packed snow of the road.

It was so cold that his first breath turned to iron in his throat, the hairs in his nostrils webbed into instant ice, his eyes stung and watered. In the faint starlight and the bluish luminescence of the snow everything beyond a few yards away swam deceptive and without depth, glimmering with things half seen or imagined. Beside the dead car he stood with his head bent, listening, and there was not a sound. Everything on the planet might have died in the cold.

Indecisively seeking help, he walked to the top of the next rise, but the faintly darker furrow of the road blurred and disappeared in the murk, the shadows pressed inward, there was no sign of a light. Back at the car he made the efforts that the morality of self-reliance demanded: trying to see by the backward diffusion of the headlamps, he groped over the motor feeling for broken wires or loose connections, until he had satisfied himself that he was help-less. He had known all along that he was.

His hands were already stung with cold, and around his ankles between low shoes and trouser cuffs he felt the chill like leg irons. When he had last stopped, twenty miles back, it had been below zero. It could be ten or fifteen below now. So what did he do, stranded in mid-journey fifty miles or more from his destination? He could hardly go in for help, leaving the sample cases, because the right rear door didn't lock properly. A little jiggling swung it open. And all those drugs, some of them designed to cure any-thing — wonder drugs, sulfas, streptomycin, aureomycin, penicillin, pills and antitoxins and unguents — represented not only a value but a danger. They should not be left around loose. Someone might think they really *would* cure anything.

Not quite everything, he told the blue darkness. Not a fouled-up distributor or a cranky coil box. Absurdly, there came into his mind a fragment of an ancient hymn to mechanical transport:

> If she runs out of dope, just fill her up with soap
> And the little Ford will ramble right along.

He saw himself pouring a bottle of penicillin into the gas tank and driving off with the exhaust blowing happy smoke rings. A mock-heroic montage of scientific discovery unreeled itself — white-coated scientists peering into microscopes, adjusting gauges, pipetting precious liquids, weighing grains of powder on miniscule scales. Messenger boys sped with telegrams to the desks of busy executives. A group of observers stood beside an assembly line while the first tests were made. They broke a car's axle with sledges, gave it a drink of the wonder compound, and drove it off. They demolished the carburetor and cured it with one application. They yanked loose all the wires and watched the same magic set the motor purring.

But here he stood in light overcoat and thin leather gloves, without overshoes, and his car all but blocked the road, and the door could not be locked, and there was not a possibility that he could carry the heavy cases with him to the next farm or village. He switched on the headlights again and studied the roadside they revealed, and saw a rail fence, with cedars and spruces behind it. When more complex gadgets and more complex cures failed, there was always the lucifer match.

Ten minutes later he was sitting with the auto robe over his head and shoulders and his back against the plowed snowbank, digging the half-melted snow from inside his shoes and gloating over the growing light and warmth of the fire. He had a supply of fence rails good for an hour. In that time, someone would come along and he could get a push or two. In this country, in winter, no one ever passed up a stranded motorist.

In the stillness the flames went straight upward; the heat was wonderfully pleasant on icy hands and numb ankles and stiffened face. He looked across the road, stained by horses, broken by wheel and runner tracks, and saw how the roadside acquired definition and sharp angles and shadows in the firelight. He saw too how he would look to anyone coming along: like a calendar picture.

But no one came along. Fifteen minutes stretched into a half hour, he had only two broken pieces of rail left, the fire sizzled half floating in the puddle of its melting. Restlessly he rose with the blanket around him and walked back up the road a hundred steps. Eastward, above jagged trees, he saw the sky where it lightened to moonrise, but here there was still only the blue glimmer of starlight on the snow. Something long buried and forgotten tugged in him, and a shiver not entirely from cold prickled his whole body with goose flesh. There had been times in his childhood when he had walked home alone and been temporarily lost in nights like this. In many years he could not remember being out alone under such a sky. He felt spooked, his feet were chilled lumps, his nose leaked. Down the hill, car and snow swam deceptively together; the red wink of the fire seemed inexpressibly far off.

Abruptly he did not want to wait in that lonely snow-banked ditch any longer. The sample cases could look after themselves, any motorist who passed could take his own chances. He would walk ahead to the nearest help, and if he found himself getting too cold on the way, he could always build another fire. The thought of action cheered him;

he admitted to himself that he was all but terrified at the silence and the iron cold.

Locking the car doors, he dropped his key case and panic stopped his pulse as he bent and frantically, with bare hand, brushed away the snow until he found it. The powdery snow ached and burned at his fingertips. He held them a last moment to the fire, and then, bundled like a squaw, with the blanket held across nose and mouth to ease the harshness of the cold in his lungs, he started up the road that looked as smooth as a tablecloth, but was deceptively rough and broken. He thought of what he had had every right to expect for this evening. By now, eight o'clock or so, he should have had a smoking supper, the luxury of a hot bath, the pleasure of a brandy in a comradely bar. By now he should be in pajamas making out sales reports by the bedlight, in a room where steam knocked comfortingly in the radiators and the help of a hundred hands was available to him at a word into the telephone. For all of this to be torn away suddenly, for him to be stumbling up a deserted road in danger of freezing to death, just because some simple mechanical part that had functioned for thirty thousand miles refused to function any longer, this was outrage, and he hated it. He thought of garage men and service station attendants he could blame. Ignoring the evidence of the flooded carburetor, he brooded about watered gas that could make ice in the gas line. A man was dependent on too many people; he was at everybody's mercy.

And then, on top of the second long rise, he met the moon.

Instantly the character of the night changed. The uncertain starlight was replaced at a step by an even flood of blue-white radiance. He looked across a snow meadow and saw how a rail fence had every stake and rider doubled in solid shadow, and how the edge of woods beyond was blackest India ink. The road ahead was drawn with a ruler, one bank smoothed by the flood of light, the other deeply shadowed. As he looked into the eye of the moon he saw the air shiver and glint with falling particles of frost.

In this White Christmas night, this Good King Wenceslas night, he went warily, not to be caught in sentimentality, and to an invisible audience he deprecated it profanely as a night in which no one would believe. Yet here it was, and he in it. With the coming of the moon the night even seemed to warm; he found that he could drop the blanket from across his face and drink the still air.

Along the roadside as he passed the meadow and entered woods again the moon showed him things. In moonlight openings he saw the snow stitched with tiny perfect tracks, mouse or weasel or the three-toed crowding tracks of partridge. These too, an indigenous part of the night, came back to him as things once known and long forgotten. In his boyhood he had trapped and hunted the animals that made such tracks as these; it was as if his mind were a snowfield where the marks of their secret little feet had been printed long ago. With a queer tightening of the throat, with an odd pride, he read the trail of a fox that had wallowed through the soft snow from the woods, angling into the packed road and along it for a little way and out again, still angling, across the plowed bank, and then left a purposeful trail of cleanly punched tracks, the hind feet in line with the front, across the clean snow and into the opposite woods, from shadow across moonlight and into shadow again, mysterious.

Turning with the road, he passed through the stretch of woods and came into the open to see the moon-white, shadow-black buildings of a farm, and the weak bloom of light in a window.

His feet whined on the snow, dry as metal powder, as he turned in the loop of drive the county plow had cleared. But as he approached the house doubt touched him. In spite of the light, the place looked unused, somehow. No dog welcomed him. The sound of his feet in the snow was alien, the hammer of his knuckles on the door an intrusion. Looking upward for some trace of telephone wires, he saw none, and he could not tell whether the quivering of the air that he thought he saw above the chimney was heat or smoke or the phantasmal falling frost.

"Hello?" he said, and knocked again. "Anybody home?" No sound answered him. He saw the moon glint on the great icicles along the eaves. His numb hand ached with the pain of knocking; he pounded with the soft edge of his fist.

Answer finally came, not from the door before which he stood, but from the barn, down at the end of a staggered string of attached sheds. A door creaked open against a snowbank and a figure with a lantern appeared, stood for a moment, and came running. The traveler wondered at the way it came, lurching and stumbling in the uneven snow, until it arrived at the porch and he saw that it was a boy of eleven or twelve. The boy set his lantern on the porch; between the upturned collar of his mackinaw and the down-pulled stocking cap his face was a pinched whiteness, his eyes enormous. He stared at the traveler until the traveler became aware of the blanket he still held over head and shoulders, and began to laugh.

"My car stopped on me, a mile or so up the road," he said, "I was just hunting a telephone or some place where I could get help."

The boy swallowed, wiped the back of his mitt across his nose. "Grandpa's sick!" he blurted, and opened the door. Warmth rushed in their faces, cold rushed in at their backs, warm and cold mingled in an eddy of air as the door closed. The traveler saw a cot bed pulled close to the kitchen range, and on the cot an old man covered with a quilt, who breathed heavily and whose closed eyes did not open when the two came near. The gray-whiskered cheeks were sunken, the mouth open to expose toothless gums in a parody look of ancient mischief.

"He must've had a shock," the boy said. "I came in from chores and he was on the floor." He stared at the mummy under the quilt, and he swallowed.

"Has he come to at all?"

"No."

"Only the two of you live here?"

"Yes."

"No telephone?"

"No."

"How long ago did you find him?"

"Chore time. About six."

"Why didn't you go for help?"

The boy looked down, ashamed. "It's near two miles. I was afraid he'd . . . "

"But you left him. You were out in the barn."

"I was hitching up to go," the boy said. "I'd made up my mind."

The traveler backed away from the stove, his face smarting with the heat, his fingers and feet beginning to ache. He looked at the old man and knew that here, as at the car, he was helpless. The boy's thin anxious face told him how thoroughly his own emergency had been swallowed up in this other one. He had been altered from a man in need of help to one who must give it. Salesman of wonder cures, he must now produce something to calm this over-worried boy, restore a dying man. Rebelliously, victimized by circumstances, he said, "Where were you going for help?"

"The Hill place. They've got a phone."

"How far are they from a town?"

"About five miles."

"Doctor there?"

"Yes."

"If I took your horse and — what is it, sleigh? — could someone at the Hills' bring them back, do you think?"

"Cutter. One of the Hill boys could, I should say."

"Or would you rather go, while I look after your grand-pa?"

"He don't know you," the boy said directly. "If he should wake up he might . . . wonder . . . it might . . ."

The traveler grudgingly gave up the prospect of staying in the warm kitchen while the boy did the work. And he granted that it was extraordinarily sensitive of the boy to know how it might disturb a man to wake from sickness in his own house and stare into the face of an utter stranger. "Yes," he said. "Well, I could call the doctor from the Hills'. Two miles, did you say?"

"About." The boy had pulled the stocking cap off so that his hair stood on end above his white forehead. He had odd eyes, very large and dark and intelligent, with an expectancy in them.

The traveler, watching him with interest, said, "How long have you lived with your grandfather?"

"Two years."

"Parents living?"

"No, sir, that's why."

"Go to school?"

He got a queer sidling look. "Have to till you're sixteen."

"Is that the only reason you go?"

What he was trying to force out of the boy came out indirectly, with a shrugging of the shoulders. "Grandpa would take me out if he could."

"Would you be glad?"

"No, sir," the boy said, but would not look at him. "I like school."

The traveler consciously corked his flow of questions. Once he himself had been an orphan living with his grandparents on a back farm; he wondered if this boy went as he had gone, knocking in imagination at all of life's closed doors.

The old man's harsh breathing filled the overwarm room. "Well," the traveler said, "maybe you'd better go finish hitching up. It's been thirty years since I harnessed a horse. I'll keep an eye on your grandpa."

Pulling the stocking cap over his disheveled hair, the boy slid out the door. The traveler unbuttoned his overcoat and sat down beside the old man, felt the spurting weak pulse, raised one eyelid with his thumb and looked without comprehension at the uprolled eye. He knew it was like feeling over a chilling motor for loose wires, and after two or three abortive motions he gave it up and sat contemplating the gray, sunken face, the unfamiliar face of an old man who would die, and thinking that the face was the only unfamiliar thing about the whole night. The kitchen smells, coffee and peanut butter and the moldy, barky smell of wood from the woodbox, and the smell of the hot range and of paint baking in the heat, those were as familiar as light or dark. The spectacular night outside, the snowfields and the moon and the mysterious woods, the tracks venturing out across the snow from the protective eaves of firs and skunk spruce, the speculative, imagining expression of the boy's eyes, were just as familiar. He sat bemused, touching some brink as a man will walk along a cutbank trying to knock loose the crumbling overhang with an outstretched foot. The ways a man fitted in with himself and with other human beings were curious and complex.

And when he heard the jingle and creak outside, and buttoned himself into the overcoat again and wrapped his shoulders in the blanket and stepped out into the yard, there was a moment when the boy passed him the lines and they stood facing each other in the broken snow.

It was a moment like farewell, like a poignant parting. Touched by his pressing sense of familiarity and by a sort of compassion, the traveler reached out and laid his hand on the boy's shoulder. "Don't worry," he said. "I'll have someone back here right away. Your grandfather will be all right. Just keep him warm and don't worry."

He climbed into the cutter and pulled over his lap the balding buffalo robe he found there; the scallop of its felt edges was like a key that fitted a door. The horses breathed jets of steam in the moonlight, restlessly moving, jingling their harness bells, as the moment lengthened itself. The traveler saw how the boy, now that his anxiety was somewhat quieted, now that he had been able to unload part of his burden, watched him with a thousand questions in his face, and he remembered how he himself, thirty years ago, had searched the faces of passing strangers for something he could not name, how he had listened to their steps and seen their shadows lengthen ahead of them down roads that led to unimaginable places, and how he had ached with the desire to know them, who they were. But none of them had looked back at him as he tried now to look at this boy.

He was glad that no names had been spoken and no personal histories exchanged to obscure this meeting, for sitting in the sleigh above the boy's white upturned serious face he felt that some profound contact had unintentionally, almost casually, been made.

For half a breath he was utterly bewitched, frozen at the heart of some icy dream. Abruptly he slapped the reins across the backs of the horses; the cutter jerked and then slid smoothly out toward the road. The traveler looked back once, to fix forever the picture of himself standing silently watching himself go. As he slid into the road the horses broke into a trot. The icy flow of air locked his throat and made him let go the reins with one hand to pull the hairy, wool-smelling edge of the blanket all but shut across his face.

Along a road he had never driven he went swiftly toward an unknown farm and an unknown town, to distribute according to some wise law part of the burden of the boy's emergency and his own; but he bore in his mind, bright as moonlight over snow, a vivid wonder, almost an awe. For from the most chronic and incurable of ills, identity, he had looked outward and for one unmistakable instant recognized himself.